THE
Lizzie AND Belle
MYSTERIES

DRAMA AND DANGER

First published in Great Britain in 2022 by Farshore

An imprint of HarperCollins*Publishers*
1 London Bridge Street, London SE1 9GF

farshore.co.uk

HarperCollins*Publishers*
1st Floor, Watermarque Building,
Ringsend Road Dublin 4, Ireland

Text copyright © 2022 Joanna Brown and Storymix Limited
Illustrations © 2022 Simone Douglas

The moral rights of the author and illustrator have been asserted.
A CIP catalogue record for this title is available from the British Library

ISBN 978 0 0084 8525 2
Printed and bound in the UK using 100% renewable electricity
at CPI Group (UK) Ltd
1

Stay safe online. Any website addresses listed in this book are
correct at the time of going to print. However, Farshore is not
responsible for content hosted by third parties. Please be aware
that online content can be subject to change and websites can
contain content that is unsuitable for children. We advise that
all children are supervised when using the internet.

MIX
Paper from
responsible sources
FSC™ C007454

This book is produced from independently certified FSC™ paper
to ensure responsible forest management.

For more information visit: www.harpercollins.co.uk/green

THE
Lizzie AND Belle
MYSTERIES

DRAMA AND DANGER

J. T. WILLIAMS
ILLUSTRATED BY SIMONE DOUGLAS

KENWOOD HOUSE

HAMPSTEAD HEATH

THEATRE ROYAL

ST GILES

COVENT
GARDEN
MARKET

STRAND

ST MARGARET'S
CHURCH

WESTMINSTER
ABBEY

SANCHO'S
TEA SHOP

TOWER
OF LONDON

ST PAULS
CATHEDRAL

RIVERSIDE
SOUTH

LONDON

Prologue

We the Lions …

My mother says that until the lions have their own storytellers, the story of the hunt will always glorify the hunter.

She has a proverb to suit most situations. She says that proverbs are 'jewels from the ancestors' to guide us through the challenges of life.

I can definitely see myself as a lion.

I am strong. As strong as anyone my age.

I am fast. Superfast, some say. No one I've met can outrun me.

I am loyal to my pride. My family – my mother, my father, three sisters and a brother – are my world.

For every proverb my mother offers, my father has a quotation.

'All the world's a stage!' he claims. 'And all the men and

women merely players!'

He believes that we each have a role to play in the great drama of life. That different situations call for different performances. The important thing is to be true to oneself in each performance.

Am I a performer? Or a storyteller? Can I be both? The heroine of my own story?

Mama says that if we don't tell our own stories, someone else will do it for us. And if we let them do that, how can we trust them to tell it right?

Until the lions have their own storytellers, the story of the hunt will always glorify the hunter.

When this story began, almost everything I knew about the world I had learned from my parents. These events changed that forever.

I decided to write them down so that I could be a storyteller for the lions.

I did not yet know that this was the story of a hunt.

ACT I

Chapter One

To begin with, there was nothing out of the ordinary about the night of Friday 11th April 1777. It was just like any other Friday night in Covent Garden. Or so it seemed. The market square swirled with street traders selling flowers and fruit in all colours of the rainbow. Coaches and carriages passed back and forth, stopping every now and then to let the horses drop their manure. Shoppers hurried along the cobblestones, pulling their coats tighter about them as the sun sank slowly behind the skyline of colonnades and spires that graced the Thames.

If someone had been looking very carefully, however, they might have noticed a tall, cloaked figure, skulking in a shadowed doorway as the crowds passed by. If they had continued to pay close attention, they might have seen the figure disappear into the back door of the Theatre Royal at Drury Lane.

Someone extremely perceptive would have also observed a smaller figure – a girl – leaving Madame Hassan's Haberdashery on Maiden Lane, clutching a package and scurrying through Covent Garden Market as though her life depended on it. And if they had followed that girl, they would have seen her tearing down the Strand, along Whitehall and into Charles Street, making a beeline for Ignatius Sancho's Tea Shop.

Right. So, I should let you know that that girl is me. Lizzie Sancho, twelve years old, Londoner. I am definitely not your typical eighteenth-century girl. *Who is?* I hear you ask. But what I mean is, I'm not interested in attending society balls or wearing the latest fashions or reading the gossip columns in the newspapers. And personally, I don't know many girls that are interested in those things. But then, maybe I don't move in the right circles.

I spend most of my time helping out with the family business. We own a grocery store in the heart of Westminster that doubles as a tea shop and what my father likes to call a 'literary salon'.

And here he is! May I present Ignatius Sancho? Gentleman. Grocer. Writer. Composer. Abolitionist.

He used to work as a butler for an aristocratic family and he knows a lot of people. I mean, a *lot*. Actors, artists, writers, musicians: you name it! The shop is always crammed with people huddled in corners, swapping stories, planning protests, hatching plots, reciting poetry, sharing secrets. A proper hotbed of news and information.

Helping out in the shop is how I have developed my extraordinary powers of observation. You see, I have a trick – a gift, Mama calls it – of noticing things that other people don't. I can tell all sorts of things about someone just by the way they enter a room, or eat an apple, or ask me for directions in the street. You'd be amazed at what you can learn about life just by observing people closely. And eavesdropping, of course.

But I digress. Back to Papa.

So, his latest obsession is acting. He quotes Shakespeare at me and our family on a daily basis – sometimes hourly, no joke.

'Everything one could wish to learn about human behaviour,' he announces, 'we could learn from William Shakespeare!'

Tonight he will take to the stage to play Othello at the Theatre Royal, Drury Lane. Othello is one of Shakespeare's very few Black characters. A military general, respected by his colleagues and those he commands, and married to Desdemona, a young white woman. The play is almost one hundred and eighty years old, and has been performed many times, but the character of Othello has yet to be played by a Black man on the British stage. Can you believe it?

When Papa first told me that, some months back, I actually thought I'd misheard him. In fact, I accidentally spat out my tea.

'What?' I spluttered, spraying tiny drops of hot water in a shower of surprise.

'Never once yet, dear Lizzie,' Papa replied, in his rolling baritone. 'Until now.'

I mopped the table surreptitiously with my sleeve. 'But that's ridiculous, Papa! Why not?'

'That, dear heart, is a very good question,' he replied, refilling my cup with Orange Pekoe tea. 'A very good question indeed.'

Chapter Two

To return to my tale, the grand bell of St Margaret's Church was striking five when I arrived at the shop. I took a moment to catch my breath and pushed open the door. Like a cheeky response to the sombre church tones, the familiar silver tinkle of the bell that hung above the door frame announced my arrival. The tea shop was toasty warm after the snappy chill of the evening air.

'Lizzie? Lizzie, is that you back?'

My mother's sing-song voice rang out from the back room. In she came, resplendent in an indigo brocade gown, her nimble-fingered hands fixing the last pins into her coiled crown of silver-and-black hair. Her large eyes shone like obsidian in the sculpted planes of her face; her umber skin glowed with health.

Mama. Strong and elegant as a queen, there was a soft

grace about her, a warmth inside her strength that made you want to cuddle up and hear her tell you stories in the sparkling Caribbean lilt of her voice. I found my mother impossibly beautiful.

She moved swiftly as she spoke, gathering up the sheets of music and script that were scattered over the counter, clearing away the breeches, blouses and bonnets that had been flung to all corners of the room. Each word chimed clear: strung together, they flowed like music.

'Lizzie, you're late, girl. You got your father's gift?'

I unwrapped the handkerchief I had bought Papa as a good luck present from Madame Hassan, the Egyptian seamstress. An exquisite, white cotton square with a motif of golden flames around the border.

'Oh Lizzie, it's beautiful!' Mama lifted the delicate fabric to inspect the intricate embroidery. 'Your father will love it! But come on, quick, now! You must wash and dress for the theatre. Your dress is hanging up in the back room. Leaving in ten!'

'What?' said a voice from the far corner of the room. 'Mama! There's no way I'll be ready in ten minutes!'

My sister Mary, fifteen, was seated at a small harpsichord, frantically scribbling notes on manuscript paper with a small quill. She shared my father's musical genius, and in addition to composing and performing on harpsichord and violin, she was obsessed with learning the dance steps that were currently sweeping the assembly halls and pleasure gardens. Papa had invited her to compose the music for the production of *Othello*, and now she was adding last-minute changes to her score.

'I wouldn't worry. There's no way we'll be leaving in ten minutes.'

That dry voice? Frances. Seventeen – the eldest of the five of us. Nose in a book, legs up on a footstool, feet crossed at the ankle. If it could be learned from a book, there was a fair chance that Frances knew it already. Now she was peering at me over the top of her glasses. 'You'll take at least four minutes to wash and another seven to get dressed, Lizzie.'

Rude. I'm not a fussy dresser, you understand; I just find girls' clothes very – fiddly. All those layers and buttons and ribbons and . . . well, it's time-consuming to say the least. When I can get away with it, I prefer to wear breeches. This evening was not one of those occasions.

And Frances was not yet done. 'By the time you're dressed, Billy will need to use the chamber pot – that's three minutes (if we're lucky) – and by the time that's done, Mary will have lost her spectacles – again. I predict at least one and a half minutes before she realises that they are on her head, and by the time we're actually out of the door . . . I give it fifteen minutes from now. Unless, of course, Billy needs to sit *down* on the pot. In which case make it half an hour.' She put her nose back into her book.

Behind her were Kitty and Billy, chasing each other round in a circle. One boy, one girl. It would have been easy to mistake them for twins. But Billy was three years old, and Kitty was five. Ill health had slowed Kitty's growth and she was no taller than our baby brother – or 'Smiler' as we liked to call him. But she was fearless and playful and full of affection for us all, which she dished out in the form of hugs and very wet kisses. They ran in the staggering circles of small children: giggling, breathless, giddy.

'Kitty! Billy!' Mother warned. 'No showing your father up on his special night, you hear me? This, my ducks, could be the most important night of his career. Standing still now!'

Mama only warned once. Kitty and Billy stopped and stood stock still, mock statues, each wobbling on one leg, trying not to laugh.

'And as for you, girls?' Mama added. 'Help me to clear up this mess as quickly as you helped to make it.'

I slipped into the back room. Our house was next door to the shop, but with just one room downstairs and two bedrooms upstairs – one for my parents plus the little ones, the other for us three girls – the shop's back room doubled up as extra living space.

There, against the bookcases, hung my dress for the

theatre: a gown of rich deep-blue, hand-stitched, with gold lace scallops around the hem, the cuffs and the squared neckline. *That sounds beautiful,* I can hear some of you saying. But the truth is, I am virtually allergic to wearing dresses. I find them irritatingly tight, maddeningly uncomfortable and pretty much impossible to run in. And I run a *lot*. But Papa had asked his friend Mrs Templeton the seamstress to make matching outfits for the family for this special occasion, declaring it was 'the African way'!

Papa is extremely proud of his African heritage and takes every opportunity to ensure that people know it. Mama is an African Caribbean woman, free born here in England. My siblings and I were all born in London. However, we are – as Papa so often reminds us – an African family.

So, on this occasion, I swallowed my reservations about wearing a fancy dress, scrubbed up quickly and put the dress on, because I knew how important this evening was to the dearest, funniest, kindest man I knew.

Chapter Three

Thirty-one minutes later, the Sancho women – plus Billy – stepped out into the London night. Mama took up the centre of the family line, Kitty in her arms. Frances walked next to Mama, with Billy in hers. I walked next to Mama too; Mary walked next to Frances. Dressed in matching indigo satin gowns and cloaks, Billy in breeches and waistcoat, we strolled proudly through the lamp-lit streets as they filled up with fellow theatregoers.

The Theatre Royal was a grand palace in the heart of Drury Lane. Papa called it 'the jewel in London's crown'. Crowds gathered under its stone colonnades, their voices fizzing with excitement and anticipation, and my heart swelled to think that my father was at the centre of it all! That in just a few moments, all these people would be watching him perform on stage!

Mary hurried straight into the auditorium to deliver her last-minute changes to the musicians and Mama disappeared to find the lady selling the playbills so that we could have a souvenir of the evening. She returned both outraged and triumphant.

'A penny a playbill! And no family discount! But I got us a good deal. I bought us an orange each, and the playbill came free!' Mama was queen of the bargain hunters.

The auditorium was a hive of sound and a riot of vision! A thousand voices twittered and buzzed around us. My skin thrilled with anticipation. How could one room be so vast? A great domed ceiling, painted with sky and clouds, appeared to float high above our heads. Proud pillars rose up and met in vaulted arches decorated with elegant carvings of fruit and flowers, angels and animals. The theatre was like a magnificent temple.

The stage, for now, was empty. As though it were waiting for something.

Above it, a hundred wax candles burned in a chandelier that glimmered like a giant crown.

But the crowd! The walls were lined with rows of people, festooned in silks and satins, purples and pinks, greens, blues, yellows: a feast of colour and ornaments! Gowns flashed and rustled. Wigs, dotted with flowers or draped with ribbons, towered above their wearers. People leaned their heads together to whisper behind fans or pass comment behind palms.

Everyone talked at once. Everyone was watching everyone else. Once we were settled in our box – a cross between a private room and a balcony – I consulted the playbill.

THEATRE ROYAL, DRURY LANE, COVENT GARDEN

ON FRIDAY 11TH APRIL, 1777
will be performed a TRAGEDY, called

OTHELLO

as written by WILLIAM SHAKESPEARE.

Directed by MR DAVID GARRICK, manager of the Theatre Royal
assisted by MR DOMINIC GREENWOODE

CAST

OTHELLO, the Moor of Venice, a General	IGNATIUS SANCHO
IAGO, a soldier, Othello's ensign	WILLIAM ASH
DESDEMONA, wife to Othello	MARY ROBINSON
CASSIO, Othello's lieutenant	RICHARD STEVENSON
RODERIGO, suitor to Desdemona	EDWARD LEWIS
EMILIA, wife to Iago, lady's maid to Desdemona	SUSANNA LAMONT

STAGEHANDS TOM JOHNSON, PUCK PATHAK
With new music composed by MARY SANCHO

On this occasion the stage will be illuminated with near one thousand candles, thanks to a generous donation from LORD MANSFIELD, LORD CHIEF JUSTICE

The doors will open at half after five o'clock, the performance to begin at half an hour after six.

It was too exciting! I leaned forward for a better look, chin in hands. Mary gave a little gasp of wonder as a young conductor with a shock of wavy red hair took his place at the front of the orchestra and the buzz of gossip quietened to curious murmurs. The musicians were poised, instruments ready, all eyes on the conductor. He bowed to the audience, turned to face the musicians and raised his long-fingered hands. The audience fell silent.

The violins started a light and steady dance up and down their scales; a cello marked a steady beat below. A harpsichord spun sounds like a web of golden gossamer. I glanced across at Mary. She was transfixed, her face the very picture of rapture, her foot lightly marking time beneath the indigo taffeta of her skirt. Her hands danced miniature patterns in the air as though she too were conducting. Frances had snuck in a copy of the playscript and was reading it behind a fan. Her foot also tapped in perfect time to the beat. Kitty and Billy sat, open-mouthed. Every one of us was under a spell.

And then the action began. Soldiers Iago and Roderigo stalked about the stage, speaking of their hatred for Othello and hatching a plot against him. According to Papa, Iago was 'the villain of the piece, consumed with jealousy'. I watched, spellbound, as Iago crept around Roderigo, his voice low and insinuating, his words winding a serpentine spell around us all.

'*I am not what I am . . .*'

In the second scene, Papa made his grand entrance. Dressed in a red velvet cloak, he strode on to the stage, every inch a powerful military general. The rich scarlet looked splendid against his mahogany complexion. Mama had cut his coils so that they sat close to his round head. His voice, deep and sonorous as a double bass, rolled over the heads of the crowd in waves of profound sound: soothing, magical.

'*For know, Iago, but that I love the gentle Desdemona . . .*'

I thrilled with pride. Papa – the star of the stage!

I was blissfully lost in the wonder of the words, when all of a sudden, I had a strange sensation – a feeling that I was also being watched.

I turned instinctively towards the watcher. Was it a version of myself I was seeing? There, on the other side of the theatre, sitting between an elderly man and a lady with a beehive of silver hair, was a girl. A girl of about my age, looking straight at me and not altogether unlike me. Her skin was deep brown, almost as dark as mine, and the tight curls of her hair were gathered up into a bun on top of her head. Her delicate face was framed by a fringe of tightly curled ringlets. She wore a gown of cream lace, the sleeves puffed at the shoulders, and a delicate silver chain around her neck. She was staring directly at me. As our eyes met, so did, it seemed, our thoughts.

I nodded.

She nodded back, smiled.

I returned her smile, lost for a moment.

And then, without warning, she suddenly looked up towards the drape of curtain above the stage. Fear flickered across her face. I followed her gaze upwards. A tall human shape hovered at the edge of the balcony above, just visible behind the curtain. And then, it vanished in a movement as quick and fleeting as the flap of a bat wing.

The girl looked back at me, stricken with horror. In the same moment, the actor playing Iago looked up too – and leaped across the stage, straight into my father. The two of them staggered and tumbled to the floor as the chandelier plummeted to the stage with an almighty crash, landing in the exact spot where Papa had been standing, sending splinters of wood flying in all directions!

The actors froze, like miniature cut-out figures in a paper peepshow. The theatre held its breath. Fear hung in the air.

The chandelier lay like a great shipwreck in the centre of the stage, smoke from its candles drifting eerily towards the ceiling.

Beside it, stretched out, motionless, lay my father.

Chapter Four

And then – pandemonium! Shrieks of panic erupted across the crowd as people rushed and scrambled to get out of the building. I turned to Mama, who was already on her feet, clutching the little ones tightly to her and craning her neck to keep sight of Papa.

Mr Ash knelt beside Papa, talking to him, shaking him gently, putting his ear to his mouth, as though to check he were breathing.

At the edge of the stage, two men were exchanging agitated, anxious words. Garrick and Greenwoode. Garrick, a sturdy man in a russet frockcoat, strode to the front of the stage, gesturing for the audience to take their seats. He had a natural air of authority about him, as though he were used to being listened to.

Greenwoode, a thin man with a long, melancholy face,

knelt down, aghast, by Papa stretched out on the floor. Poor Papa!

'Quiet please, quiet please!' Garrick cried, clapping his hands until the din subsided to a ripple of murmurs. He pulled out a handkerchief and patted it across his brow. 'Ladies and Gentlemen! Please! This is a most unexpected and unfortunate turn of events. I urge you to leave the building in the same civil, orderly and gentle fashion in which you entered. For now, we must attend to our honourable colleague Mr Sancho. We will investigate and post news as soon as we are able. But for now, you must leave peacefully; please. I bid you goodnight.'

The little ones were wailing loudly. Mama thrust Billy into my arms and pushed Kitty towards Frances.

'Girls,' she said, agitated but determined. 'I need you to be strong now and go home without me, so that I can see to your father.' She fished around urgently in her purse and thrust two heavy coins into Mary's hands. 'Mary. Go out into the street and find a coach to take you all home. I'll be there with Papa as soon as I can.'

We pushed our way through the crowd as it jostled and spilled out into the street. I held Billy fast to my chest, pressing his head into my neck so that he did not have to see the chaos milling around us. A wave of panic rose up within me. Knowing I had to stay calm for my baby brother,

I steeled myself against it.

Outside, the air bubbled with rumour and speculation, a greedy buzz of voices clamouring for news too soon.

'A near tragedy! – What an event for opening night! – Do you suppose he's dead? – It's the height of drama! – and in front of his family too – it's too terrible to think about!'

Mary stood in the road, desperately trying to flag down a coach. Some ignored her completely and rolled on past. Others slowed as they passed but were swiftly commandeered by well-to-do theatre guests more adept than us at getting what they wanted. I jiggled Billy around in my arms, trying desperately to comfort him and stop his crying.

Frances strode over to Mary and grabbed the coins. She waved them high in the air with one hand, placed two fingers of the other to her mouth and gave out a searing whistle. In an instant, a coach swerved over to the kerb and stopped in front of us.

Mary jumped in and I passed Billy to her. Frances followed with Kitty. I hesitated on the pavement, scanning the crowd anxiously for the girl I had glimpsed in the theatre. My mind was racing. Where was she? Surely she had seen the shadow on the balcony too?

And just as my mind spoke that thought, there, moving swiftly through the crowd towards me, was the girl in the cream dress, a violet cloak covering her hair and shoulders.

'I do hope your father is not hurt! Come tomorrow morning if you can!' she whispered in my ear as she pressed a small card into my hand and flew past me.

I spun around to see her take the elderly gentleman's hand and follow the silver-haired lady into a coach waiting across the street. The coachman cracked his whip; the horses snapped into action and surged forward. Confused and curious, I stared helplessly after them as the coach carrying the mysterious girl in violet pulled away from the chattering crowd and vanished into the star-studded night.

Chapter Five

It felt strange arriving home to an empty shop. The ashes in the fireplace were cold and a damp chill had settled into the house in our absence. It clung to the walls and furniture like an unwelcome guest.

Mary set about lighting the candles in the kitchen. Each one bloomed into a golden halo and brought the corners of the room into view around us.

Papa's spectacles lay neatly folded on the counter. His chair by the hearth, conspicuously empty. On the kitchen table, the handkerchief I had bought him. How could I have forgotten to take him his good luck present? My heart was pierced with a sharp stab of regret, as though tonight's events were in some part due to my carelessness.

Frances went straight upstairs with Kitty, who had fallen asleep in the coach on the way home. I walked around the kitchen, jiggling Billy in my arms. He rubbed his eyes fretfully, resisting sleep without Mama to comfort him. Frances came back downstairs and fetched some milk from the cellar to warm for him.

Mary sat down at the harpsichord but did not play. Frances paced up and down while the milk heated. Not one of us had yet spoken a word, but I knew we were all dreading the same thing.

When the milk was ready, I sat down on the floor with my legs crossed and cradled Billy in my lap, tipping the cup to his thirsty lips. I watched him guzzle it down greedily, his soft-lashed eyelids sweeping up and down, up and down, down, down, as he sank into a milk-drunk sleep. My fear for Papa grew more powerful; questions about the chandelier seared my brain.

'Frances . . .' My voice was small in the dim gloom of the room. 'Will all be well with Papa?'

She stopped pacing and spun around to face me, her face contorted with her own fear. 'How should I know, Lizzie? I didn't see any more than you did!'

Her harsh words stung. My eyes felt hot.

She softened. 'Oh, Lizzie, I'm sorry.' She joined me on the floor, putting her arm about my shoulder with a sigh. 'I want to be able to tell you that everything will be well, but the truth is, I don't know. At least Mama is with him.'

'Papa's strong,' said Mary, with determination, as if to convince herself. 'He'll be fine. When it's his time to go, it will take more than a fall.'

I wished for Mary's faith, but I could not shake the image from my mind of Papa lying so still on the stage, Ash bent over him, shaking him.

I blinked the thought away. It was too painful.

Billy stirred in my arms. I stroked his warm forehead, and he sighed a feather-soft breath back into sleep. I decided to hold Mary's reassuring words in my heart while we waited for Mama to arrive home.

A few hours later, a coach pulled up outside the shop. Frances rushed to open the door. In they came together, Papa leaning heavily on Mama, one arm around her shoulders, his head bandaged.

'Papa!' Mary cried.

With Billy fast asleep in my lap, I could only watch as Mary and Frances threw their arms around him, yet I thought my heart would burst with relief!

Though his face was drawn with exhaustion, his eyes danced at the sight of us.

'Girls, dear girls, you . . . you need not have waited up!'

He spoke with an effort, his voice laden with weariness. 'I am quite well. It seems I have suffered a mild concussion – it is of no serious concern.'

'Ignatius!' Mama's voice was all anxiety laced with warning. 'We talked about this in the carriage. You *will* take this seriously. Doctor Phipps was very clear. You hit your head when you fell to the floor. You *must* rest yourself.'

She caught sight of me on the floor in the corner and smiled sadly.

'Lizzie!' she said. 'You got Billy to sleep? Good girl! Can you bring him up? Mary, give her a hand. Frances, help me take your father up the stairs . . . I'll watch him closely tonight. And then to bed, girls. It's been a difficult day. You'll all need some decent sleep before tomorrow.'

Chapter Six

I awoke with a jolt, head and heart beating like drums. Daylight bathed the room. My sisters' beds were empty, their sheets pulled tight into the neat rectangles Mama insisted on. Muffled voices floated up the stairs; beneath them, the familiar sounds of movement in the kitchen. Breakfast. Distant notes fell like blossoms from the family harpsichord.

My sleep had been troubled, broken by nightmares. The sight of my father almost crushed to death by a chandelier had haunted me throughout the night. He called out my name, but I too was stuck somehow, unable to move towards him, unable to help. Through the wreaths of smoke that curled up from the stage, the girl in the violet cloak appeared before me, her dark eyes holding a deep sadness. I reached towards her; the girl turned away.

Dreams and reality met and merged in my mind. What

on earth had happened last night? I reached under my pillow and found the calling card the mysterious girl had pressed so insistently into my hand.

On one side was a fine illustration of a grand house high on a hill, flanked by trees. On the other side, in an elegant, sloping script, the words:

Lord and Lady Mansfield
Kenwood House
Hampstead Heath
London

Was she a Lady, then? A young Lady Mansfield? Of African birth? Whoever she was, she had asked me to visit her. And she had certainly seen whatever I had, there above the stage.

'Breakfast, Lizzie!'

Frances' voice pulled me from my thoughts. I unwrapped the satin scarf holding my hair in place and washed and dressed quickly.

Mama and Mary sat side by side at the harpsichord, their

eyes fixed on the music manuscript, their hands working in harmony. The halting notes of their gentle duet were a calming counterpoint to the boisterous sellers' cries that sailed in from the street outside.

Frances stood at the hearth making the hot chocolate. The white apron she wore over her dark cotton dress was a sign that she was in charge of family breakfast this morning. She pushed a wooden spoon in wide circles around a cast-iron pot bubbling with hot milk and ground cocoa. I watched as she sprinkled in cardamom and cinnamon. The sweet spices filled the room with a glorious heady aroma. So familiar, it calmed my spirits a little.

Kitty and Billy sat – or should I say wriggled – together at the table, each dipping a hunk of bread into a steaming bowl of hot chocolate.

'Mmmmm!' they hummed as they dipped and ate, giggling through hamster cheeks stuffed with chocolatey bread.

I sat down beside Kitty, my insides rippling with anxiety. The handkerchief lay open on the table, a reproach. I folded it carefully and wrapped it once more in its pocket of golden silk. Poor Papa.

The bell above the door sounded. It was Mercury, with the day's newspapers.

'Morning, Mrs Sancho! Morning, girls! All right, Billy?'

Billy giggled and kicked his legs under the table.

When Mercury was around, Billy never took his eyes off him.

Swift, fast-talking and reliable, Mercury ran all over London, delivering newspapers and taking messages for extra coins. His real name was Kofi, but his speed had earned him his nickname, after the Roman god of messages. He had a cheeky sense of humour, and I enjoyed having a boy of my own age to run around the city with. One of our favourite pastimes was to go down to the riverside and race along its banks. Mercury was the only person I had ever met who could match me stride for stride. For that alone, I had great respect for him.

We squeezed each other in our usual tight hug of greeting.

'Here, Lizzie, everyone's talking about what happened at the theatre last night! Front page news in the *Daily Advertiser*! Send my best wishes to your papa . . .'

I took the paper from Mercury's outstretched hand. The silver locket he wore on a bracelet on his wrist sparkled in the morning sunlight. A gift from his mother. It was all he had left of her. Aside from his friends, Mercury was pretty much alone in the world.

I shook open the folded newspaper. There was a picture of Papa on the front page. Not a brilliant likeness, I noted.

'Catch you same time tomorrow!' Mercury called, grabbing a bread roll from a bowl on one of the tables – an unspoken treat always on offer from Mama for him – and pulling the shop door closed behind him. I watched as he fixed his cap and set off up the street to finish his deliveries, his newspaper bag slung over his shoulder.

The Daily Advertiser

DISASTER AT DRURY LANE!
Curtains for *Othello*?
African grocer-turned-actor injured in near-fatal accident!

Disaster struck at the Theatre Royal, Drury Lane yesterday on the opening night of David Garrick's new production of *Othello*, starring Ignatius Sancho, an African.

Local grocer Sancho was set to play the famous Black general but was injured when a large iron chandelier plummeted from the ceiling, leaving audiences reeling in shock. Sancho would have been crushed, if not for fellow actor, Mr William Ash, who sprang across the stage to move Sancho out of harm's way.

During his fall, however, Sancho hit his head, suffering a mild concussion.

Mr Garrick is known for his experimental stage designs and extravagant lighting choices.

Assistant Director Dominic Greenwoode said, 'This is a most unfortunate accident. Of course we take the safety of our actors very seriously. We are conducting an internal investigation into the incident and will be speaking to our stagehands Tom and Puck to get to the bottom of this. We regret to announce that the performances of *Othello* must be cancelled until we can ensure that the stage is safe again.'

Mr Garrick is, it seems, more optimistic in his outlook, saying, 'Mr Sancho is recovering from this unfortunate accident, and we hope to resume rehearsals within the week. *Othello* is set to be the theatrical production of the decade!'

If the production goes ahead, Sancho, a long-standing friend of Garrick's, will be the first African to take on the role.

So the official story was that this had simply been an accident. There was no mention whatsoever of the figure on the balcony. But I had seen someone, and I was certain that the girl watching me at the theatre had seen them too. Had no one else?

'You're late up, sister,' Frances said gently, as she placed a bowl of hot chocolate on the table and sat down opposite me. She held my hand in hers and I took comfort from its warmth.

'Morning, Frances.' I sipped the chocolate. 'Thank you. But where's Papa?' My brain was foggy. He had come home last night, hadn't he?

'Your father's resting in bed, Lizzie,' Mama explained.

'He's had a terrible shock. We're all going to need to pull together to look after him.'

'Could I take him some hot chocolate please?'

'You can take up a cup by all means, but don't wake him if he's asleep.'

Chapter Seven

Upstairs, Papa was lying on his back, his eyes closed, the round mountain of his body heaving in the gentle rhythm of sleep. The bandage around his head was stained with a small spot of blood near the left temple.

'Papa?' I whispered.

He opened an eye. 'Is that you, Lizzie? Come, dear heart.'

With difficulty, he pulled himself up to a sitting position and I set the chocolate down on the table next to the bed. I arranged a pillow behind his back and climbed up beside him, curling up under his left arm as I used to do when I was younger. He winced as I settled against him.

'Does it hurt, Papa?'

'A little, my sweet. But Dr Phipps will return to see me and will no doubt bring some relief for my pain . . .'

Dr Phipps was a local apothecary who had cared for our

family for many years now. An elderly man with colourless eyes and long white hair that spread over his shoulders, he ran a shop on Neal Street, in the Seven Dials district, where the medicine people and herbalists sold their remedies for healing.

'I was really worried about you, Papa.'

Papa squeezed my shoulder and spoke softly. 'There, there. No matter, Lizzie. What's done is done. It was a terrible accident. But no one was seriously hurt . . . we must thank heaven for small mercies.'

'So you think it was an accident then?'

'But of course!' He shrugged. 'I fear the chandelier was too heavy for the ceiling. Some over-ambitious set design, no doubt. Garrick will speak to the stagehands.'

Puck and Tom were responsible for looking after the props and costumes and helping to move the stage sets around. I knew Puck well. When Papa was busy in rehearsals, we would practise sword-fighting with the props in the costume cupboard. Papa said that Puck had been given his name after playing Puck in a sailors' performance of A Midsummer Night's Dream. The part of the mischievous sprite seemed to have been written for him, Papa had said. He knew every inch of the theatre and every whisper of gossip.

Tom kept himself to himself. He was a couple of years older than me but at least a foot and a half taller.

I had said hello to him on a couple of occasions, but he had just lowered his head and pushed past me down the corridor. Now I thought of it, he had never once spoken a word to me.

I made a mental note to speak to them both as soon as I had the chance.

I didn't want to press my suspicions on to Papa. Didn't want to suggest to him that someone might have wanted to hurt him – or worse. But I could not bear the thought on my own. I had to discuss it with the girl I had seen at the theatre. Like me, she had seen something for sure.

'What will happen to the play, Papa? The newspaper says that the performances are cancelled.'

'Well, my hope is that as soon as the stage is fixed, the show can go ahead. Of course your mother is insisting I rest for a few days, but I am writing to Garrick to let him know that I am keen to return to the theatre as soon as possible.'

He patted my hand reassuringly.

'Garrick is a good friend: he knows how important this performance is. Not just for me of course, but for all our African brothers and sisters who want to see a Black man in a lead role on the stage. We must establish our presence on a public platform! We have so many fine actors, performers and musicians among us, as well you know.'

It was true. Every month, Papa and his friends hosted

and performed at the Black dances of the London parks. Musicians, dancers, poets and actors shared their talents in the circle, taking it in turns to bring their skills into the round and entertain the crowds.

'Next, we will be writing our own plays, our own poetry, our own novels!' Papa continued. 'Think of all the different stories that we could write about our own lives. All the different roles waiting for us in the wings . . .'

He was right. Why did we never see ourselves on stage? It did seem odd now that Papa pointed it out. That was Papa, always thinking ahead.

This had to be a good moment to give him his present.

I took the small parcel out of my pocket.

'For luck, Papa. Though I wish I had given it you yesterday!'

'Lizzie, dearest,' he said softly as he took it from me. His face shone with pleasure.

'I had it made especially,' I said eagerly, as he opened up the silk wrapping. 'By the Egyptian lady at Maiden Lane.'

He unfolded the handkerchief and gently ran his thumb over the golden flames stitched into the fabric. 'There's magic in the web of it,' he whispered.

'She makes them to order!' I said, delighted that he seemed to love his gift. 'You can choose a motif to match your name so that it feels like it belongs to you and you alone.'

You see, my father was born on a slave ship as it made its way from the coast of West Africa to the Caribbean Sea. His mother died before it reached shore. His father leaped from the ship, flew on the breeze for a fleeting moment of freedom before being swallowed by the waves. In the small city of Cartagena, on the northern coast of Colombia, Papa was baptised Ignatius by a Spanish bishop. Ignatius means flame.

Papa gathered me up in the tightest of hugs and said, 'Thank you, my dear, thoughtful child! I shall keep it safe.'

He folded it carefully, tucked it into his shirt pocket and placed his hand over it, as though for protection.

'Tell Frances, the chocolate's delicious,' he said, as I got up to leave. 'I hope she's made enough to serve for shop breakfast. Here at home, the show must go on!'

Downstairs, Mama was sitting at the table with Frances and Mary. She dismissed the little ones so that they could get down and play and gestured to me to come and join my sisters. I had a hunch that she was going to make an important announcement.

'I was just saying to your sisters, Lizzie, that we need to keep our spirits up for Papa and help him to make a speedy recovery,' she said. 'Last night was a shock for everyone – especially for him. If he's to get back on his feet and return to work any time soon we must stay positive. And we need to be organised. While he's resting, we'll take it in turns to look after him and to run the shop.'

She rolled out a large scroll of paper. 'I've made up a rota.'

A wave of sighs fluttered around the table.

Mama pretended she had not heard us and tapped the rota firmly with her finger. 'Saturday. Lizzie, it's your turn to go to the market today. You're already late and we're running low on candles and flour. Then you have your Letters lesson with Papa. He can't write but he can still speak. It'll help keep his spirits up while he rests.'

'What?'

Mama pulled her head back sharply and raised her eyebrows, which was customary Ann Sancho-speak for: *You might want to think again before you make that face / use that tone of voice with me, young lady!*

'I'm sorry, Mama,' I said quickly. 'Truly. Only, I . . . I was hoping to visit a friend this afternoon.'

Mama folded her arms. 'Let me remind you of a few things, Elizabeth.'

Elizabeth! She really did mean business.

'This weekend, my girl,' Mama continued, 'I will be running the weekly accounts, taking stock of the shop supplies, serving in the shop, and looking after your brother and sister. Your father is ill, you hear me? And you want to go visiting a friend? You offer me a problem like that, you need to offer the solution too, y'nuh?'

I should probably point out at this stage that my mother was the business brain of the family. She drew a tough line when it came to discipline, but thanks to her entrepreneurial spirit, she could sometimes be open to negotiations.

'How about I swap my day with Frances, please?' I said. 'I'll take on an extra market day to make up for it, take care of Papa's correspondence and do a double Letters lesson tomorrow!'

Mama sat back to consider my offer. Her expression told me she was impressed.

Frances, however, was not. 'What! Why should I have to swap and do the market today?'

Mama turned her razor-gaze on my sister. 'Frances? You have something you'd rather do?'

Frances rolled her eyes and snapped her book shut. 'All right, all right. I'll walk you over to your friend's, Lizzie, and I'll go to the market for you. But you owe me one. Or two, strictly speaking.'

'Thank you, Frances. Thank you, Mama! I'll be home by six, I promise!' I grabbed Mama and kissed her cheek. It was soft, warm.

'Home by *five*, Lizzie. And you *must* come home safely. Frances will meet you halfway. And double Letters tomorrow!'

Mama retained her stern look while issuing her instructions, but as she waved us away, a hint of a smile broke through, just enough to reveal the little gap between her front teeth that she frequently told us was a sign of good fortune.

Chapter Eight

Frances and I stepped outside into the bustling street, jumping back immediately to avoid the wooden wheels of a cart piled with cauliflowers as it clattered past. The morning was bright and chill, the cobbled streets alive with people pushing carts and barrows, carrying bundles and baskets, shouting invitations to buy, weaving in and out of the path of the horse-driven traffic that thundered up and down the road around us.

'So, spill the beans!' said Frances, looping her arm through mine as we marched along.

'What?'

'Come on! You can't get anything past me. I know you too well. What on earth are you up to?'

I should have known that Frances had an ulterior motive for agreeing to escort me. I looked around to make sure no one was watching or listening, reached into my dress pocket for the embossed visiting card and handed it to Frances. It felt like sharing a magical secret.

'Look!' I whispered.

'Good gracious!' Frances laughed. 'Where on earth did you get this?'

'It was given to me, I'll have you know! By a girl I met at the theatre. She told me to come and see her as soon as I could.'

'Did she, now?' said Frances, clearly surprised. 'Right. Well, if it's Kenwood House you're headed for, we'd better get a move on. I can walk you as far as the south end of Hampstead Heath, but you'll need to go on from there on your own if I'm to get home with Mama's supplies any time before tomorrow. Still, I am impressed! Rubbing shoulders with Dido Belle!'

'With who?'

Frances stopped walking. 'Dido Belle. You do know who she is?'

Well, obviously I didn't, but Frances was always making me feel as though I didn't know about things and people that I should. Matters on which she was, of course, an expert. That said, she shared my gift for reading people and so immediately saw right through my hesitation.

'Dido Belle is the great-niece of Lord and Lady Mansfield,' she said.

I shrugged. The name rang a bell . . .

'Lord Mansfield – Lord Chief Justice! The most eminent lawmaker in all of England? Some say he has more power than the king himself!' Frances marched on, leaving me alone for a moment with the drama of her announcement.

Right, so I had heard of Lord Mansfield. He cropped up in conversations in the tea shop, and I had met him once, briefly.

'Dido Belle is his niece?' I asked, running to catch up with Frances.

'Exactly! This is what I've been trying to tell you!'

We paused for a moment before crossing Oxford Street, where the horses and coaches were muzzle to wheel, so this required some concentration. As we proceeded up Tottenham Court Road, Frances continued:

'The Mansfields don't have any children of their own, but their two great-nieces live with them: Dido and Elizabeth. Dido's father is Captain John Lindsay. He's an officer in the Royal Navy. They say that during a trip to the Caribbean, he met an African woman, Maria Belle. She was enslaved, just like Papa was as a child.'

We slowed our steps and walked in silence for a moment at the memory of our father's painful childhood.

'Some say Lindsay's crew freed her and her people, but the details are hazy, to say the least,' Frances said after a while. 'Anyway, John and Maria got together. They had a baby.'

'Oh!' Embarrassing. Move on.

Frances smiled, clearly enjoying the feeling of knowing more than me about these matters. 'Anyway, the baby girl, Dido, was placed in the care of her great-aunt and uncle. So she lives with them at Kenwood. I don't know where her mother is. Mama would know more.'

I could not believe Dido's extraordinary story. Could not believe that a girl, of African descent, just like Frances, Mary and me, was living in one of the finest country houses in the land. I knew that there was something intriguing about her! Now I had to know more.

'How do you know all this, Frances?'

I was genuinely bemused.

She waved her hand dismissively. 'Oh, you know. Newspapers, gossip columns . . . and I keep my ear to the ground . . . when you're a teenager, you'll understand, but until then . . .' She winked and tapped the side of her nose.

Argh! It was only months until I was thirteen, but everyone treated me as though I was the baby of the family!

Frances turned me to face her for her usual last-minute inspection. Ever since I was tiny, Frances had always made sure that I looked 'ready' to meet someone. She insisted on me looking what she called 'presentable'. I called it 'the check'. I wondered how old I would be before she decided that I was old enough to have the final say on my own appearance. Fifteen? Twenty-five? Seventy? She tucked a stray curl back into one of my two thickly twisted braids and brushed away a piece of fluff from my crimson cloak.

'Right, I need to leave you here, Lizzie, if I'm to get to the market,' she said. 'Thanks for that! The house is on the other side of the Heath, on top of the furthest hill – you can't miss it! Just keep heading northwards and upwards.' She waved in the direction of a high wooded hill. 'See you get a lift around the Heath later in the family carriage. I'll meet you here at three, so that we can be home by five like Mama said. And for helping you out today, I expect no less than an invitation to tea at Kenwood House!'

We embraced. I watched as my sister walked back towards Haverstock Hill, straight-backed, head held high, hips gently swaying to a secret music. Frances, in so many ways the sensible one in the family, never ceased to surprise me.

As I stepped on to the Heath, the golden green of a lush meadow stretched up and away before me. Sheep dotted the fields: squat and woolly they stood, staring sleepy-eyed, jaws chewing in slow circles. Indigo butterflies swooped and flitted among the gently waving grasses. My heart sang at the sight of it. An oasis of calm, just on the edge of the city! How had I never been here before? I took a deep breath, gathered up my skirts and my spirits and started the steep climb up the hill.

Chapter Nine

The walk to Kenwood House was longer than I anticipated. The path I had followed led me into a dense wood, and before long, trees towered around me on all sides. Heavy with ancient wisdom, they bent and swayed with a slow grace, whispering and shushing as the breeze brushed through their leaves. Shafts of white sunlight pierced the tree canopy in dusty, diagonal beams.

I pressed on, holding my skirts above my ankles as I tramped through the tangled mess of damp undergrowth. Was I even going in the right direction? I knew I should be heading north, but the huddled trees obscured my view of the sky and the path seemed to have disappeared among the brambles.

Thorns and prickles caught on my cloak and my skirt, slowing me down. There was no one in sight. The wood thickened around me. The breeze blew colder. Fear crept like a vine around my heart. What if I were lost? Surely these woods could not go on forever? I looked back over my shoulder, wondering whether I should turn back.

A trill of birdsong sounded above my head. A robin? It came again, somewhere to my left. A sweet and clear fluting sound. I followed it; surely I was almost there?

At last, the trees gave way and I emerged from the wood into the early afternoon sunshine. The tiny brown bird fluttered off into the sky. In front of me, a clear lake sparkled and a wooden bridge led to a soft slope of green that swept upwards to – Kenwood House! A magnificent building of pale golden stone crowning the crest of the hill, sunlight glinting off its arched windows. Proud and serene it stood, like a creamy iced wedding cake against an azure sky.

Spurred on by a wave of relief, I crossed the bridge and sprinted up the grassy slope, encouraged by the excitement of knowing that I would soon meet with Dido Belle. I followed the path around the side of the house to a stone courtyard. There, between two columns, was a large black door, grander than any door I had ever seen.

A lion's face snarled in brass.

I glanced down at my mud-caked boots and the dirt-splashed hem of my dress. My cloak was covered in sticky burrs from where I had pushed my way through the dark bushes. Now that I was on the doorstep of what looked to me like a palace, something inside me shrank.

Papa's soothing voice drifted into my mind. *'Remember, Lizzie, it is not clothes, nor possessions, nor riches, but manners that maketh the man!'*

Or woman, Papa.

I gathered up my courage and lifted the door knocker, banging it three times hard. At first, silence. Then the measured tap of footfall on polished floor.

The door was opened by a tall, young, African man, dressed in the red livery of a coachman. He held his head high, his shoulders back, and his face was set in a serious expression. His eyes, though grave, held kindness.

On seeing me, he nodded and stepped back, indicating with a smooth sweep of the arm that I should enter.

I thanked him and crossed the threshold into a grand hall. It seemed to hold a hundred histories within its walls. Paintings stared down at me from all around. A vast chandelier hung, sparkling sharply, from the centre of the ceiling. My heart caught for a moment as the image of Papa lying motionless on the stage flashed in my mind.

'You're here! You came!' Dido Belle's voice sang with delight as she sailed into the Hall. She was dressed in pale-yellow taffeta, with matching satin slippers on her feet. Her hair was combed out, a glorious ebony coily mass sitting just above her shoulders.

I felt a rush of warmth to see her, but as she approached me, my relief was chased away by butterflies. This grand palace was actually her home.

At the sight of the coachman, Dido steadied herself to a walk. 'Thank you, Joshua,' she said gently, as he lifted the cloak from my shoulders.

Unsure of what to say, I simply nodded my thanks.

'I've been watching out for you all day!' Dido said, thrusting a pair of grey satin slippers towards me. 'I saw you approaching from the window in my room. I chose these especially, to match your dress,' she added coyly.

I looked down and saw that I had decorated the polished wooden floor with a crooked trail of muddy footprints from the front door to the middle of the hall where I now stood.

'Oh! I – I'm so – Oh no!' My cheeks grew hot and I quickly grabbed my left foot in my hand to pull off my boot, hopping around in the other and making a little circle of mud to adorn my first piece of artwork.

Brilliant. Just the impression I wanted to make.

Joshua caught me by the elbow to steady me.

'Oh! . . . Thank you . . . sir.'

(You understand, I was not used to having an adult wait on me, let alone calling him by his first name, as Dido had done. Mama would be horrified. If I were to call him Joshua, I would at least be expected to prefix it with 'Uncle' or 'Master'.)

Dido was still holding out the delicate slippers towards me, but now my hand was covered in mud and I was pulling off the second boot and glancing around for some kind of magic trapdoor so that I could do a disappearing act and come back tomorrow to try again. Or not come back at all?

'Here, allow me,' she said, dropping to her knees to place the slippers on my stockinged feet.

I wobbled elegantly first on one foot, then the other. Meanwhile, Joshua shook out a handkerchief, wiped down my hands and removed my offending boots in what seemed like one swift gesture . . .

This was not the first meeting I had pictured.

Dido stood up, her cheeks a little flushed, and stepped back to admire her handiwork.

'There! It is so good to see you again,' she said breathlessly. She had dimples when she smiled.

My voice caught in my throat.

There was an awkward pause before she spoke again.

'And how is your dear Papa? I read in the newspapers that he banged his head?'

I swallowed hard and found my voice. 'Er, yes, he's well, thanks . . . considering. He's concussed. Shocked. Tired. But he hopes to be back on stage within days.'

She raised her eyebrows with a smile, then squeezed my hands – a reassurance. 'He sounds like a survivor! I am glad of it!' The smile gave out to a sudden laugh. Bright, joyous. 'I don't even know your name!'

Of course. Why would she? My name had not, like hers, appeared in the newspapers.

I took a deep breath and drew myself up proudly in the way that Mama had taught me to do when I introduced myself. 'Lizzie,' I said. 'My name is Lizzie!'

She smiled again. 'I'm thrilled to meet you, Lizzie! I'm Dido. But you can call me Belle.'

Chapter Ten

I had never seen such opulence in a place that someone I knew called home. The walls were covered from floor to ceiling with gilt-framed paintings. Portraits of men in armour or fur-trimmed robes, women draped in silk and satin, rose-cheeked children playing with small dogs. A world very different to the one I lived in. Each person appeared so contented, so serene, so pleased with themselves. Was that how they really felt, I wondered, or was it a pose for the painter?

'Who *are* all these people?' I whispered, as we made our way down the corridor, arm in arm.

'Uncle William and Aunt Betty collect artworks,' explained Belle. 'Some of these people are family, some of them are Royals.'

'Family? As in *your* family?'

Belle hesitated. 'Yes . . . yes, I suppose so. On my father's side. I live here with my great uncle, my great aunt and my cousin Eliza. Of course, *they* are my family. But the people on the walls . . .'

We fell into an awkward silence. It all seemed so strange to me.

'Now,' Belle went on, brightening, 'I want to show you something.'

She walked ahead of me and pushed open a large set of double doors to reveal a grand chamber.

'The library!' she announced, spreading her arms wide as she walked the circle of the room.

Along one wall, three large windows ushered in a flood of sunlight. The ceiling soared above us, blue like a spring morning sky, swirling with ornate white patterns of leaves, flowers and ferns. Everywhere I looked, the walls were covered with books: their leather spines – red, green, brown – lined up next to one another, on shelf after shelf. In my own family, books were sacred objects. I stepped across the threshold; my skin tingled.

High columns flanked each end. An immense gilt-framed looking glass hung on one wall – it held all the mystery and magic of a fairy tale, as though it might speak to me at any moment. The windows framed a view of the slope I had raced up to get here. Beyond the slope, two dazzling swans glided along the glassy surface of the lake, elegant and ink-eyed.

I followed Belle slowly around the room, trailing my finger over the spines of the books. *The Complete Works of William Shakespeare*. *Gulliver's Travels* by Jonathan Swift. *A Dictionary of the English Language* by Dr Johnson. *The Life and Opinions of Tristram Shandy, Gentleman* by Laurence Sterne. Sterne! Papa and Sterne were great friends. Sterne visited the shop regularly to take tea and they wrote letters to each other often.

There was *Oroonoko* by Aphra Behn – a play by a young white Englishwoman about an African prince. *Poems on Various Subjects Religious and Moral* by Phillis Wheatley. Phillis Wheatley! Taken from her family in West Africa and sold into enslavement in America at the age of seven, she had grown up in Boston, writing poetry. She had come to London when I was eight years old to publish her first volume of poetry at the age of just nineteen. In our house, she was quite a hero.

Looking at Belle's books, I thought of our beloved bookcase at the back of the shop. Something inside me relaxed.

'My father would love this place!' I said. 'His books mean everything to him! And he writes letters . . . endlessly! He once told me that writing letters was like talking on paper.'

'Yes!' Belle exclaimed. 'I often think of books that way, too. As though someone, no matter how far away, no matter how long ago, is sharing their thoughts with me through their writing. Talking to me through the words on the page. When I read their words, I hear their voice.'

This thought hung sparkling in the air for a moment between us.

It was Belle who broke the silence. 'I've been going over what happened last night, Lizzie. In fact, I hardly slept for worrying about it.' A shadow seemed to move through her thoughts. 'I think I saw someone on the balcony above the stage just moments before the chandelier fell. And I believe you saw it, too?'

'Yes!' I said. 'But it seems no one else did. My father's convinced that the chandelier fell by accident. And that's what the papers are saying, too!'

We sat down together on a chaise longue in the bay of the window.

Belle shook her head. 'It was such a fleeting glimpse. But someone was definitely up there. And . . . and something strange occurred earlier that evening.'

I felt my blood rising. 'What happened?'

Belle stood and paced the room, her hands working over one another. 'Well, Uncle, Aunt and I travelled to the theatre by carriage. My cousin is away at school in France at the moment, so it was just the three of us. Joshua drove us there. We arrived early, as Uncle wanted to get into the theatre before the crowds arrived. Aunt Betty was excited about the play.'

Here she suddenly looked rather coy.

'She reads your father's letters in the newspapers and holds him in very high esteem – but Uncle William was distracted. He was buried in some papers he had brought with him from his study.'

She went on, walking through the events in her mind.

'As our carriage pulled up to the theatre, it stopped suddenly with such a jolt that we were all thrown from our seats. In fact, the carriage nearly overturned! Uncle was furious, and I could hear Joshua shouting at someone in the street. He's usually very calm, so I noticed it. When I looked out of the carriage window, I saw them slipping into the back doorway of the theatre. They must have run straight out in front of our horses!'

'Did you see their face?'

'No, I didn't. They were hooded, and I only saw them from behind. I noticed how tall they were, though. We were all four of us troubled by it: such an intrusion on a special occasion!'

'What time was this?' I asked.

'Just before five,' Belle replied decisively. 'I remember

because the bells rang five just as we got out of the coach. But then later, in the auditorium, the music – your sister's music! – soothed our spirits. It was so beautiful, Lizzie. So stirring.'

She wandered to the window, gazed out at the swans on the lake.

'I felt as though I were listening to a distant memory, or the sound of a dream. In fact, it made me think of my mother. I imagine she would have been very proud to see your father on stage.' Belle paused here, leaned her head against the window's cool glass.

She sighed, then turned her disarming smile on me.

'And then, in that very moment, I saw you. You see, Aunt Betty and Uncle William are extremely kind. They love me very much. And believe me, I do realise how incredibly lucky I am to live here. It's beautiful. The house, the woods, the lake.'

She played absent-mindedly with the locket at her throat. 'But my days are quiet. My cousin, Eliza – well, all she thinks about at the moment is who will be attending the next society party, who she might marry. To be honest, I rarely meet with anyone my own age. And I've certainly never been introduced to another Black girl before. So you see, I couldn't quite believe it when I saw you. I thought I was dreaming. But . . . out of the corner of my eye, I saw that strange shadow on the balcony, just behind the curtain. And then they were gone! And the chandelier falling like that. It was horrible!'

There was no doubt about it. This was no accident. Someone had deliberately tried to hurt my father. I did not want to worry him by sharing my fears, as the production meant so much to him. In my mind, the best way to help him was to find and unveil the culprit as quickly as possible. We had to move fast.

'Can you meet me at the theatre tomorrow?' The memory of my double Letters lesson snagged at my excitement. 'Or Monday? I can offer to collect some of my father's things for him from his dressing room. We can investigate the balcony, talk to the stagehands? I know one of them, Puck. He must have seen something, and he would definitely help us.'

Belle looked hesitant. 'Do you think it's wise to jump straight in? If we alert the culprit to our suspicions, won't we be putting ourselves in danger?'

'But we're losing time as it is!' I said. 'I say we start investigating straight away. What if they plan to strike again?'

Belle pressed her lips together and nodded. 'All right, then. I can ask if Joshua can drop me off!' She smiled shyly. 'As for this evening, would you like to stay for dinner?'

Dinner?

'Oh good grief! What time is it?'

How could I have so completely lost track of time?

'Just coming up to five o'clock . . .'

'Oh no!'

My promise to my mother, my deal with Frances. Both forgotten, ruined.

'I'm so late!' I jumped to my feet and started towards the door. 'I've got to get home!' My parents would be desperately worried. And once their worries were allayed, they would be furious! It would take me another two hours to get across the Heath.

Belle was already on the other side of the room, pulling on a large golden cord. A distant bell sounded throughout the house. 'I'll ask Joshua to take you home. He won't mind, I promise. And Nancy who works in the dairy can come with you as a chaperone.'

As I climbed into the waiting carriage, Belle closed the door and smiled at me through the window.

'I felt the same way, you know,' I said, pulling up the hood of my cloak. 'When I first saw you. I couldn't believe it. It's brilliant that we've met, Belle!'

'At the theatre on Monday, then?' Belle asked, beaming.

'At the theatre on Monday!' I called as Joshua snapped the reins into action.

I turned to the back window of the carriage and watched Belle walk back up the path to the house. My new friend seemed to get smaller and smaller as the coach pulled away. It struck me how alone she looked as she disappeared into that splendid house and closed the magnificent black door behind her.

ACT II

Chapter Eleven

That I had arrived home in one of London's smartest carriages, driven by an African gentleman and accompanied by a chaperone, did not spare me the pepper-hot wrath of my mother. Where exactly had I been all this time and who was this friend and could I not have sent word and did I not think – for one second! – about how worried she might have been as if she did not have enough to worry about already and did I think that at twelve years of age I knew everything and was old enough to go roaming around the streets of London until all hours, 'because, young lady, you most certainly are not!'

Mama went outside to thank Joshua and Nancy for bringing me home safely, and, I was certain, to find out every last detail about where I had been and what I had been doing.

I stomped through to the back of the tea shop and slumped down at a table in a gloomy corner, grateful for somewhere to hide. Just because I had made a mistake on this occasion did not mean that I was too young to look after myself. Wasn't I allowed to make mistakes?

The usual evening customers had made themselves at home. Dotted around the room, men and women huddled together at their tables, deep in conversation. Two coachmen sat silently by the fire, staring into the flames, lost in thought. A young dark-skinned woman in a green dress went from table to table, handing out pamphlets – a common sight in our tea-room.

At a table by the wall, a group of musicians from the theatre formed a tight circle around a single candle, discussing my father's ordeal.

'What a terrible thing to happen! And on opening night of all nights.'

Will, a young violinist, shaking his head in sympathy. His accent still bore the singsong traces of his early years in Antigua. I stayed very still, keen not to draw their attention to me, listening to their conversation from the semi-darkness of the corner.

'A terrible business!' added Sally, an old friend of Mama's who played the flute. She tapped the table with a finger as she spoke. 'Let's hope Garrick and Greenwoode fix the stage sharpish and make it safe! We want to see Ignatius back up there. We've been waiting a long time to see a brother take the role of Othello.'

'Well – *we* want it to happen!' observed George, the trumpet player, a large round man with a voice to match. Famed for his vocal skills, he would often drop by in the afternoons to read the newspapers aloud in the shop so that people who did not read could hear the news. 'And we know why, too. But you know how it is. I heard the usual grumbles at the market yesterday about having an African play a role written by England's greatest playwright.'

'But the character *is* an African man!' cried Will. 'Othello is a brother! Shakespeare wrote him that way!'

'And I told them that!' said George, spreading his arms wide. 'But there's some that don't like to see us in the spotlight. All fine when we're waiting on their tables and driving their coaches. Another thing when we want to take centre stage. But we *need* the visibility, man – *especially* given what we're dealing with right now.'

Will noticed me in the corner and tipped his head in my direction to signal to the others.

George waved a huge hand at me. 'Lizzie! Didn't see you there, my girl!' he said brightly, in that way adults have sometimes when they don't want you to know what they've been talking about and aren't sure how much you've heard.

'Do send our best to your father, won't you?'

'Of course, Uncle George – thank you,' I said.

As they turned back to their huddle, I stared past them out of the window, wondering why Mama was taking so long with Joshua.

There are times when our state of mind can stop us from taking in important information. Was it exhaustion or anxiety about my father that made me slow to notice someone standing in the shadows across the street, watching the shop?

A tall figure with a huge barrel chest. It was hard to see clearly through the darkness, but they were dressed head to toe in black, a mask covering the bottom half of their face. Framed by a doorway, not moving, not making a sound. Just watching. I knew that silhouette, that frame. With the recognition, panic soaked through me like iced water.

I stood abruptly, pushed past the tables of people drinking tea and telling tales and ran out into the sharp chill of the night. The figure was gone, the shop doorway empty.

I stepped out into the road and looked both ways up the street. Night had fallen and the shops and houses were all cloaked in soft ink. Even the moon was wreathed in a shroud of black cloud. All I could see was Belle's carriage disappearing up the road, and Mama walking towards me, gathering her woollen shawl about her shoulders. No sign of the figure anywhere.

Mama fixed me with an arrow-sharp look. 'So you spending time at Kenwood House now? With Dido Belle?'

'Did you see someone out here, Mama?' I said.

'You mean Joshua and Nancy? Who just drop you home?'

'No . . . someone else . . . across the street . . .'

She turned and followed my gaze to the empty doorway. 'No one else, Lizzie. Just the folks from Kenwood House. You never mention that's where you were going today.'

Had I imagined it? In the darkness and the fog it was so

hard to tell. My brain swam with exhaustion.

'And look at the state of you, girl!' Mama frowned. 'Good grief! A muddy dress! Your boots, covered – for shame!'

The fact that I had dared to present myself at Kenwood bearing signs of having walked across the Heath, bringing decades of shame raining down on our family's reputation, only added fuel to the fire. My mother continued to scold me, but my attention wandered in and out. Her voice seemed to come from far away.

What I did grasp was that I was to go 'straight to bed and be up super early' for my Letters lesson, while 'considering the consequences of my behaviour'.

I didn't protest. I was too grateful for the prospect of sleep.

Chapter Twelve

12

The Wonders of Correspondence – Eighteenth-Century Style

Perhaps in the future, people will find a way to communicate instantly, to send written messages at speed, but this is how we write to each other in 1777.

Instructions for writing a letter in the eighteenth century

You will need:
- A quill pen. (This is a large wing feather from a bird such as a goose. The word 'pen' comes from 'pinna' – the Latin for 'wing'.)
- A sheet of parchment or paper.
- Ink.
- Wax, for sealing.
- Your stamp.

Seat yourself comfortably at a writing desk – or, in my case, the table you share with the rest of your family for cooking, eating, playing card games, doing accounts, etc.

Tell your family you need some space to write. (This may have no effect whatsoever, but it's good to get into the habit of saying it.)

Think carefully about what you wish to say. (Some people like to plan their letters more than others. Father and I jump straight in, but Mama and Mary, for example, like a detailed plan.)

Have your inkwell ready and full of ink. (Take care not to spill on your paper, your clothes, the table or the floor, as this can result in staining and a great deal of fuss from one's parents.)

Dip your quill pen into the inkwell to load up with ink – gently shake off the excess drops.

As you move your hand across the page, ensure that your hand does not smudge the ink on the page.

When the ink is dry, fold the paper into an envelope.

Write the address of your correspondent on the front of the envelope so that your letter may safely reach its destination.

Seal it with wax – for privacy. This way, if the seal is broken when the letter arrives, your recipient will know if someone has tried to open the letter before it has reached them.

When the letter is ready to send, walk to the nearest collection post and wait for the post boy.

There are four posts a day.

The further away your correspondent, the longer your message will take to arrive. If I were to write to someone on an island in the Caribbean for example – let's say, Barbados – it could take up to three months for my letter to arrive by ship.

It should also be noted that the recipient pays to receive the letter, or it will not be delivered.

Eagerly await a response.

Ideally, letter-writing is a two-way activity. Hence the word 'correspondence' – which comes from the Latin meaning 'people replying to each other'.

Today in my double Letters lesson I was supposed to be writing to the newspaper about the importance of audience concentration at the theatre. Why had I agreed to such a long lesson? I watched the clock. The hands barely moved. I laid down my quill pen. All I could think about was the shadowy figure on the balcony, and outside our window. All I wanted was to get into the theatre to start investigating. I had to get to the bottom of what had happened before Papa returned to work. But if Papa was staying at home to rest, how could I justify turning up at the theatre without him?

'Post for you, Lizzie!'

Frances, standing in the doorway with a wry smile, holding in the air a letter for me!

Sunday, 13th April 1777

Kenwood House
Hampstead Heath
London

My dearest Lizzie,

What a joy it was to make your acquaintance yesterday!
It was a delight to receive you here at Kenwood. I do hope
that your visit was the first of many.

I trust that you returned home safely and that all was well
in spite of the lateness of the hour.

I am writing, sadly, to let you know that I will be unable to
join you at the theatre as hoped on Monday morning. Aunt
Eliza says I am to stay here for the morning to attend to my
lessons. I am extremely disappointed, I don't mind telling you.

I know that you are keen to begin the investigation as
soon as possible, so do please go on ahead without me, but
proceed with caution. I will join you in the afternoon.

Perhaps I could do some reading to help with the
investigation? Uncle swears by the power of books as the best
sources of information. I will explore the library to see what
I can find.

I was glad to hear that your father is making a recovery.

Do please send my kind regards to him and to your mother
and all your siblings.

I look forward to meeting with them one day in the not-so-
distant future.

Do please write back when you can!

Yours sincerely,
Dido Belle

Sunday 13th April 1777

Dear Belle,

I hope this letter finds you well, etc, etc.

Thank you so much for having me at Kenwood!

Can't believe I had not visited the Heath before. That walk across it was one of the best I have ever taken — and I walk all over London!

Ugh! Like you, I am working at home on my lessons. My sisters and I are all schooled at home by our parents. Papa teaches us Letters and Literature, Theatre Arts, Public Speaking and Music. Mama teaches Accounting, Business, Wisdom from the Elders and Dance.

To the investigation! I will visit the theatre tomorrow morning as planned and try and get up to the balcony above the stage as soon as I arrive. I'll see if I can find any clues as to who was up there that night.

When you can join me, we can start questioning the cast and crew. My friend Puck works backstage. He's bound to have useful information for us.

Yours, in haste, with warmth,
Lizzie Sancho

Sunday evening, 13th April 1777

My dear Lizzie,

Do please take care at the theatre – I have concerns about you jumping in headlong!

I have found some information which I wish to relay to you as a matter of urgency in advance of your visit to the theatre in the morning.

I have come across an interesting book entitled: Works of Architecture by the Brothers Adam.

Was this really an urgent message?

It's a collection of drawings and plans by the great architects of the age, Robert, John and James Adam. On its pages are detailed maps of buildings, sketches of doors, arches, rooftops, and illustrations of houses, streets and garden squares.

It did not seem so.

Robert Adam is the family architect. He's redecorating Kenwood House. Aunt and Uncle made arrangements for the house to be extended after my cousin and I moved in.

I had no idea what it meant to have a 'family architect' or have your house 'extended'.

The Theatre Royal, Drury Lane, was originally designed by Sir Christopher Wren

Ah! Finally, some information that meant something to me! I knew that Wren designed St Paul's Cathedral because Papa loved the sound of its bells ringing on a Sunday and we often walked past just to hear them . . .

but the architect Robert Adam made some adjustments to the theatre building two years ago. In the book is a map of the theatre. It's a rabbit warren of backstage rooms and corridors, secret passages and hidden chambers. I have copied out the map by hand and enclosed it here for you, with directions.

I seeeee . . .

To get up to the balcony above the stage, you need to find a staircase hidden away in the room labelled the Tower. At the top of the Tower is an attic room that leads to the balcony over the stage. That – is our crime scene.

I couldn't believe I had been so slow on the uptake, but I got it now.

My new friend was clearly a genius.

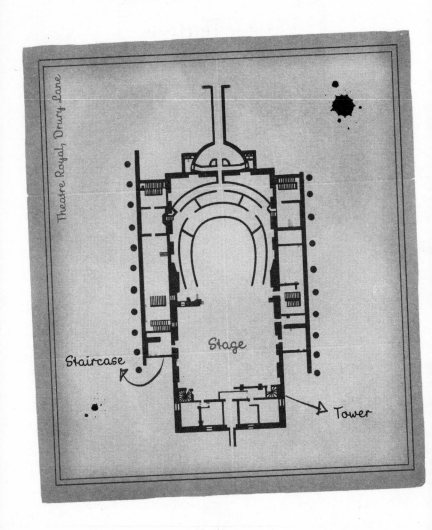

On Monday morning I rose with the lark – though the sound that actually woke me was the rooster who lived at number 25. I had spent almost the entire weekend in dresses; today was a day for breeches and that was that. I would be climbing stairs and exploring hidden spaces. I pulled on a plain pair of knee-length breeches and a white cotton shirt. Mama had agreed to my wearing these clothes for my own comfort and convenience. I folded the map that Belle had sent me and slipped it into my shirt pocket. I was set but for one thing.

How would I persuade my parents that I needed to go to the theatre?

'Lizzie!'

Mama, using the voice she used when she was about to give me an instruction I would do well to follow.

'I need you to clean and set up shop while I pop to Mrs

Thomas to see if she has a spare newspaper today. Mercury hasn't arrived with ours.'

I glanced at the clock on the mantelpiece. Ten past seven. It wasn't like Mercury to be late.

I figured the sooner I got on with my chores, the sooner I could leave for the theatre, so I set about sweeping and swabbing the shop floor. I washed the windows inside and out, wiped down the tables, broke up the sugar and prepared the table settings.

When it was time to open up, there was already a queue of morning customers gathering outside the door. I welcomed them in, watching as each person took up their regular table. Mrs Simpson, the milliner who wore the most extravagant hats, sat by the window in a circular, tilted, orange creation decorated with a black ostrich feather. She invariably ordered a pot of bergamot tea and two slices of cinnamon toast. Mr Partridge, a short, bespectacled lawyer, always took the table at the back of the room where he read all the newspapers from cover to cover, tutting loudly in between sips of his hot chocolate.

Here you were as likely to find a liveried footman as a lady of leisure, a washerwoman as a waiter. Over the years, Papa had built up a sizeable network of friends, friends of friends, and friends of friends of friends, who loved to spend time at Sancho's. A steady stream of writers, artists, musicians, coachmen, seamstresses and many more would pop in for a quick cup of tea, or make themselves at home for a few hours, ordering pot after pot, if they were at liberty to do so. All thrived on rich conversation.

Mama returned with the newspapers, accompanied by Dr Phipps, who had come to check on Papa.

'Lizzie,' he said gruffly, nodding curtly to me as he passed. I had learned by now that Dr Phipps didn't bother too much with manners, but Papa praised him as 'a most excellent physician!'

I had just finished pouring Mrs Simpson's tea when Mama came back downstairs.

'Your father has written a letter for Mr Garrick, Lizzie,' she said. 'He'd like you to deliver it directly to Mr Garrick at the theatre. You're to wait there and bring a response by return, understand?'

I nodded, barely able to contain my excitement. Papa's letter was just the excuse I needed! This gave me time to explore, no questions asked! I hung up my apron and grabbed my cloak.

'Take care, please,' Mama added. 'Stick to the busy roads and stay out of the alleyways. Remember it can be dangerous out there.'

And with that she handed me Papa's letter, gave me a swift hug and waved me off.

Chapter Fourteen

14

Inside the theatre, it was eerily quiet. The actors had been sent home until further notice, and the auditorium was empty. A great crack scarred the stage where the chandelier had landed. I shivered, wishing that Belle were here with me.

I pulled the map out of my pocket and followed the painstakingly scripted directions.

Backstage was a veritable warren of winding passageways. I crept down the north corridor to the space behind the stage, as she had instructed. There was no window back here and the little light that seeped through from the auditorium diminished with each step I took. Soon I was forced to feel my way along the wall as I proceeded into darkness.

It was a strange sensation, being devoid of sight and having to rely solely on my sense of touch. When the cool smooth surface of the wall changed to rough wood beneath my fingertips, I knew I had reached the door to the Tower. I found it unlocked. It swung open to reveal a small, circular room, at the centre of which stood a spiral stone staircase. A solitary beam of light shone down from a casement window above.

I stepped inside, leaving the door open behind me. The air was stale, and chilly as the inside of a tomb. I craned my neck to see where the staircase ended. It twisted upwards into darkness. My courage quivered.

I thought of the stories that Frances devoured during long evenings by the fire. Sometimes she would read passages aloud to us, holding a candle beneath her chin to give her face a ghoulish glow and add a tinge of terror. Gothic tales of abandoned castles and haunted abbeys. Stories of melancholy monks and gruesome ghosts, of women trapped in secret chambers, or climbing endless staircases towards terrible secrets. Women who fell into mortal danger because they were too busy reading novels – which was currently thought by many to be one of the most dangerous things a woman could do.

I climbed up through the cold gloom, taking each step with caution. The stairs wound round and up in a seemingly endless spiral. They narrowed as I ascended and I had to grip the iron handrail with both hands to prevent myself from falling.

When I reached the top, a wooden hatch blocked my way. I pushed it open and hauled myself into a room where the air was dank and chill. This had to be the attic room Belle had mentioned in her letter. Above me, the walls arched into a domed ceiling. Their greying plaster was covered in faint cracks, and I had the sensation of being inside a giant skull. At the far end of the room was a heavy crimson curtain.

The air was thick with dust. Cobwebs hung in long, low loops across the room. A solitary chair sat empty in the corner. Beneath the faint smell of damp was something drier, dirtier, but familiar. Stale tobacco. Tiny shards of light glinted in the gaps between the wooden floorboards that groaned beneath my feet.

In the centre of the floor, just this side of the curtain, the iron attachment from which the chandelier would have hung had been torn from the floorboards. I knelt down. The hole in the floor offered a glimpse on to the bare stage. Someone must have wrenched the fitting out of the wood and untied the chain that held the chandelier in place.

I pushed the curtain aside gently, and saw the auditorium, empty as a ghost-ship.

The balcony I stood on ran along the back of the stage. From here, you could hear and watch the entire performance as it went on below. You could hide yourself behind the curtain and avoid detection altogether.

On the floor, something caught my eye. A small piece of paper, tightly folded. I opened it up: it was a torn scrap.

The ink was smudged, the rest of the word indecipherable.

A noise beneath me. Footsteps. Heavy, deliberate. Someone was coming up the stairs!

I shoved the piece of paper into my shirt pocket and looked around frantically for a way out. On the far wall, two doors side by side. The footsteps slowed as their owner reached the top of the stairs. I rushed over and tried the door on the right. It was locked. I tried the other – a dark tiny cupboard, but the footsteps had stopped and now the hatch was opening, so I had no choice but to crawl inside and close the door behind me. A tiny crack in the door revealed a sliver of the room.

I held my breath. Someone was hauling themselves through the hatch as I had just done. A shadow passed across the floor. Something heavy was being dragged across the floorboards.

Why had I hidden in here, where I would certainly be found? A pair of black boots strode towards the cupboard and stopped.

'I think you had better come out of there, missy – don't you?' said a gruff voice.

Gruff, harsh – but unmistakably, a woman.

Chapter Fifteen

I pushed open the cupboard door and unfolded myself from the tiny space into which I had squeezed my limbs. My heart kicked in my chest. Sitting on a chair in front of me was a tall and powerfully built woman. Her hair was cut close to her head and she wore a loose white shirt, brown breeches and heavy black boots. Her skin was the glorious deep purple of blackberries; her golden eyes glinted like a tiger's. They sparkled with amused interest as I clambered clumsily out of the cupboard and stood before her.

'I think you need to tell me exactly what you're doing up here, don't you?'

She spoke with a slow drawl, her voice like a cat stretching out its limbs after a long sleep in the hot sun. I flitted through a mental record of accents I had heard in the shop. American?

I wiped the dust from my breeches with my hands. 'I'm just . . . looking around.'

She raised her eyebrows.

I shrugged. 'You know. Exploring . . .'

I had intended to sound nonchalant – instead I sounded deceitful.

'Exploring?' She stretched out the word as though testing it for truth. 'I see.'

Quebecois. She was Quebecois.

Her eyes scanned the room. 'And, while you were – *exploring*, did you find anything of . . . interest?'

The small scrap of paper in my shirt pocket suddenly felt like an iron weight.

'No, Ma'am.'

I had told a downright untruth. I resisted the urge to swallow.

She leaned forward and eyed me closely. 'So . . . you didn't see anything, or . . . anyone?'

She sat wide-legged, elbows on knees, hands grasping each other in a firm grip.

'No, Ma'am.'

My underarms prickled with sweat. I concentrated on keeping my breathing steady.

'So you don't have any . . . business being up here?'

Her words were firm, deliberate.

Was she threatening me? I glanced towards the staircase, trying to calculate my chances of overcoming her if she meant to hurt me or stop me from leaving. She ran her hand over her head and the muscles in her arm rippled beneath her skin. Slim, I concluded. My chances were very slim.

'You're Sancho's girl, aren't you?' she said suddenly, smiling like a cat with a mouse's tail beneath its clawed paw.

How did she know my father? Then again, most people did.

'Yes, Ma'am. Yes, I'm Lizzie.'

Surely if she knew my name it would make it harder for her to harm me?

'You're kind of tall for nine.'

That was too much.

'I'm *twelve*.'

She looked surprised, then stroked her chin thoughtfully.

'I saw you come in here, but now you need to leave. I've got work to do up here. Important work, do you hear me? You need to move along and stay out of the way. Is that understood?'

She stood, hands on hips, her shirt billowing out around her like a sailor's, the single gold hoop earring she wore gleaming against her blackberry skin.

'Yes Ma'am. And what's your name, Ma'am?'

She flashed a smile. Bright white, with a single gold tooth on one side.

'Girl! I like your style! Meg. My name is Meg. Now, let me open up the hatch for you so that you can climb on down and get yourself out of here.'

I slipped through the hatch and stepped down carefully, keeping my gaze firmly fixed on my feet.

'Don't let me catch you up here again, Lizzie!' Meg's voice ricocheted down to me like an echo in a canyon. 'It's not safe! You stay out of the way, and you stay out of trouble, you hear?'

Chapter Sixteen

16

I staggered out of the Tower and into the corridor, my legs trembling beneath me.

What would I tell Belle when she arrived? That I had used her map and made my way up to the Tower as planned, but had found nothing but a scrap of paper whose words I couldn't even make out? That instead of unearthing crucial clues as I had promised, I had ended up hiding in a cupboard from a woman who – well, I had no idea who she was!

When Belle's carriage pulled up outside the theatre, I stood awkwardly in the colonnade, wondering how to relay the disappointing news.

Her arrival had drawn quite a crowd of spectators – young women, fussily dressed in their ribboned bonnets and rustling taffeta, turning every now and then from their hushed conversations to side-eye me with disdain. As

Joshua jumped down from his seat to open the carriage door for her, I drew myself up to my fullest height. In spite of our recent exchange of letters, the last time I had seen Belle suddenly seemed very far away.

She stepped down gracefully from the carriage. Under one arm, she carried a large green leather pouch and in the other hand she held up her skirts so that the hem of her dress did not drag in the mud that clogged the street gutter. She looked exactly like what people called 'a lady'.

'Lizzie!' She waved as she made her way towards me.

The gaggle whispered behind their hands. I ignored them.

'How *is* Mr Sancho doing?' she asked loudly, taking my arm.

'Very well, thank you.' I glanced back at the whispering girls. They pushed their noses into the air and turned their backs towards me.

Once we were inside the entrance hall to the theatre, Belle heaved a sigh. 'Friends of my cousin. Ignore them. They follow me around everywhere. Sometimes I wonder whether they're just waiting for me to put a foot wrong.'

She took one look at my face and frowned suddenly. 'Lizzie! You look terrible! Whatever is the matter?'

Her concern was piercing.

I pulled her into the nearest corridor. 'I went up to the Tower. I found the balcony.'

Her eyes widened. 'So you found it!'

'Yes – the map . . . it was perfect, thank you! But . . .'

My cheeks burned as I pictured myself crouching in the cupboard, hiding from a woman in an oversized shirt.

'But – what?' Belle said. 'Did you find anything?'

'Only this.' I pulled the scrap of paper out of my pocket and showed it to her.

Belle took it from me. 'It looks like an address. 21 . . . it must be Phoebe or Phoenix something or other.'

'How do you know?'

'How many other words do you know that begin with the letters P.H.O.E.?'

Belle had a point.

'This is a brilliant start, Lizzie!' she said. 'Look, I've got something to show you too.'

She unbuttoned the leather pouch and pulled out a magazine.

STAGE DOOR MAGAZINE
The drama enthusiast's entrance into the secret world of the theatre!

I had seen copies of this magazine before. Papa subscribed to it, and I had caught Mary sliding copies off the tea-room tables to read in private when she thought no one was looking. She snuck them up to her room when she wanted to get the inside scoop on the famous musicians, dancers and actors of the day. When Mary was reading *Stage Door*, she was in another world entirely and no amount of calling could catch her attention.

'*Stage Door* is the top magazine for information on all the latest theatrical productions. It's full of juicy interviews with actors and musicians!' said Belle. It sounded as though Belle and Mary would probably get along very well. 'But look! This edition is from a couple of weeks ago.'

She opened it up to the centre spread.

'The writer's a woman. Anonymous though . . . as usual.'

Though it was well-known in writers' circles – so I had overheard in the shop – that more and more women were publishing their writings, it was currently the fashion for women to write anonymously. Sometimes they even tried to disguise the fact that they were a woman. On the one hand, I could hardly blame them. Mama had told me how hard it was for women to get their words into print compared to men. On the other hand, I couldn't help feeling that if I were to write something, I would want everyone to know it was me that had written it.

STAGE DOOR MAGAZINE

Trouble in Paradise at the Theatre Royal, Drury Lane?

by Your Mystery Correspondent

Theatre impresario David Garrick and his assistant Dominic Greenwoode are known throughout Theatreland for the stormy nature of their business partnership. This writer cannot help but notice that they find it virtually impossible to agree on anything these days. However, in spite of their fiery arguments, often conducted in public in the nearby Brown Bear tavern, the two have been firm friends for many years, working closely together on dozens of successful productions.

Garrick, our most lauded theatre director, first made his name as an extremely talented actor. His lifelike portrayals of characters such as Romeo, Hamlet and Richard III have reduced audience members to joy, tears, and fury by turn. His voice, his command of language, his talent for gesture and movement are so naturalistic that many have heralded him as the greatest actor known to date! Furthermore, he is a passionate advocate of the work of William Shakespeare and has spent time, money and resources reviving his work and celebrating his legacy.

Manager at the Theatre Royal, Drury Lane for many years, now, as Garrick nears retirement, he has decided to stage *Othello* with Ignatius Sancho – an African Gentleman – in the lead role: a casting he claims will be his swansong before he bows out of theatre life for good.

Greenwoode is by far the lesser known of the two, but he has performed in almost as many productions as Garrick, taking smaller roles to allow him to work as producer at the same time. Greenwoode also started out as an actor and has a long list of minor roles to his name, such as Bottom in *A Midsummer Night's Dream*, Sir Andrew Aguecheek in *Twelfth Night*, and Corin the Shepherd in *As You Like It*.

He hoped, for some years, to play Hamlet, but inside sources reveal that Garrick has repeatedly refused to stage the play with Greenwoode in the lead. This writer wonders whether that refusal may have created a rift beyond healing between the two men.

More news from the *Othello* production in due course . . .

'And voilà – our next move!' Belle said triumphantly. 'We speak to Garrick and Greenwoode.'

D avid Garrick and Dominic Greenwoode shared an office on the west corridor of the theatre.

The sign on the door read:

DAVID GARRICK,
DRAMATIST, DIRECTOR, THEATRICAL
ENTREPRENEUR EXTRAORDINAIRE!

ASSISTED BY DOMINIC GREENWOODE

From behind the door, two voices raised in anger wrestled with one another.

'This chandelier business is a complete disaster, I tell you! We must cancel the production – it's just too risky!'

'Nonsense! You're over-thinking things as usual, Greenwoode. It's a minor hold-up, but we can get everything fixed and shipshape in no time.'

'Someone has to do the thinking, Garrick. That shambolic opening night is the talk of London! People are calling for the cancellation of the show. If we want to save the theatre company, we need to ditch *Othello*.'

'I'm not about to cancel the entire production because of one accident! No doubt Ignatius will be right as rain soon enough and we can resume rehearsals. If he can pick himself up from this and carry on, surely we can!'

Silence. I pressed my ear to the door. Belle looked at me questioningly. I put my finger to my lips. Without warning, the door flew open, and I was caught in the utterly unmistakable position of eavesdropper.

Greenwoode. His shirt ballooning around his lean, wiry frame, his black hair tousled, his pale grey eyes alight beneath a furrowed brow. His thin red lips were pressed together in held fury. Beads of sweat glistened on his forehead.

'Ladies!' he said with more than a degree of annoyance. 'May we *help* you?'

I stood up, feeling awkward, caught out.

Belle stepped forward briskly, all smiles, her hand

outstretched. 'Mr Greenwoode! Mr Garrick! You must forgive us!' Her voice oozed confidence, sweetening the atmosphere like honey over oats. 'Miss Sancho and I are *ardent* fans of your work.'

Greenwoode looked flustered. 'Well, thank you . . .'

He shook Belle's hand reluctantly.

'Is that Mansfield's girl out there, Greenwoode?' came a sanguine voice from the back of the room. Garrick.

Greenwoode looked me over. 'And Sancho's too, by the looks of it.'

Mansfield's girl? Sancho's girl? We did have names of our own!

'Bring them in, bring them in!' cried Garrick.

Greenwoode stepped back and Belle swept past him into their office. He bowed low with an exaggerated flourish of the arm as I followed her in.

A large room, with a high ceiling. Two vast windows spilling light on to a heavy oak table. The table was littered with scribbled notes, pages of script, apple cores, two tankards full of – judging by the smell in the room – warm beer, and an assortment of quill pens. A pile of books tottered in the centre of the table: *Hamlet* by William Shakespeare, *The Revenger's Tragedy* by Thomas Middleton, *The Prince* by Machiavelli.

Garrick stood with his hands clasped behind his back.

A king surveying his kingdom.

'Lizzie! Good to see you, my dear!' he boomed.

'Mr Garrick . . .' I nodded my greeting and held my hand up in a half-wave. I didn't curtsy for anyone.

Amusement danced in Garrick's quick brown eyes. 'My, you're growing fast! Don't tell me – you must be, what, ten by now?'

Man alive.

'I'm *twelve*.'

'And Miss Dido Belle!' he exclaimed with a bow. Theatrical, of course. 'What an honour, Mademoiselle, to make your acquaintance. My compliments to Lord and Lady Mansfield.'

Belle smiled demurely, curtsied. 'And my profound compliments to you, Mr Garrick. It is a singular honour, I assure you.'

I stopped short of rolling my eyes. Why didn't people just say what they meant instead of dressing up all their words in bows and ribbons? And it was strange hearing Belle slip so easily into that talk.

'Do please assure your Uncle, Miss Belle, that all is in hand,' said Garrick. 'We are working day and night to restore the stage to its former glory so that the production can go ahead.'

Why was he reassuring Belle about the play? What about

my father? Was it safe for him to return? Shouldn't Garrick have been reassuring me?

I stepped forward. 'Mr Garrick. A letter, from my father. I'm to take him a response by return, please.'

I handed it over. We all watched as Garrick broke the wax seal and unfolded the paper. He nodded slowly as he perused the letter.

'Well, what does it say?' asked Greenwoode.

'He's keen to return to work as soon as possible!' announced Garrick triumphantly. 'He wants the show to go on! And so it shall! We are fixing the stage and the chandelier. We can open again in a matter of days!'

Days? We only had *days* to find out who had tried to drop a chandelier on my father before he returned to the theatre?

Garrick was moving things around on his desk, lifting up books, sifting through piles of newspapers. 'Ladies, if you are happy to wait a moment, I shall pen my response to that effect immediately! . . . Let's see now . . . I have writing paper just here . . . somewhere.'

'Desk drawer, right-hand pile,' said Greenwoode mournfully, walking to the window.

'Ah yes!' cried Garrick, opening the drawer and pulling out a sheet. 'I don't know what I'd do without him, isn't that right, Dominic? He handles everything for me, you know. My correspondence, the performance schedules, all the administration . . .'

I cast a glance at Greenwoode. He was standing by the window, leaning against the wall.

We all waited as Garrick penned his reply. I glanced at Belle. Her eyes were fixed firmly on Garrick. He folded the letter, sealed it with the scarlet wax and applied his stamp to the seal.

Did he really have no concerns about opening the show again? I had to know.

'But Mr Garrick – is it truly safe for my father to return?' I asked.

It was Greenwoode who spoke up. 'I've told Garrick I'm worried the theatre is not safe for Sancho! But he won't listen.'

He turned away, as if in disgust.

'He never listens,' he said with resignation, sitting down in a seat beneath the window and gazing on to the bustling street outside, before facing me then with a fierce intensity. 'Your father must have received quite a shock, don't you think? Something like that could shake you to your core. Of course, it might have been an accident, but . . .'

Might have been an accident?

What did Greenwoode know? What was he trying to tell us?

'Do you believe, Mr Greenwoode, that the chandelier

was dropped on purpose then?' I said. 'An attempt at murder?'

From across the room, Belle widened her eyes at me, as though to stop me speaking.

Garrick cast daggers from his eyes at Greenwoode. 'Now, now!' he warned, coming out from behind the desk with his hands up. He began to pace the room. The suggestion had clearly put him into a state of deep agitation. 'We should not, under any circumstances, jump to such rash conclusions! It is my belief – my firm belief! – that this *was* simply an accident. I have no reason to believe that the theatre is not safe!'

He took a breath and regained control over the rise of his emotions.

'Look . . .' He sank down into the chair behind his desk. 'It is . . . possible . . . that the chandelier was too heavy.' A flicker of guilt passed across his face. 'But we will take precautions to make the theatre safe; I give you my word! We will tone down the lighting for the performance and proceed with the show as hoped. In the meantime, my stagehands are working day and night to repair the stage. It is my hope that we can open again within the week. And I have assured your father of this in my letter.'

'Garrick! Come now!' Greenwoode's voice was harsh with urgency. 'We need to be honest with them!' He paused.

'Tell them about Tom.'

Garrick went puce with rage. 'The devil's teeth, man! Must you?'

I turned to Greenwoode. 'What about Tom?'

Greenwoode looked grave. 'Tom Johnson is – was – one of our trusted stagehands.'

I was stunned. 'Was?'

Garrick was shaking his head. 'We don't know that Tom's involved . . .'

'Indeed we don't,' said Greenwoode, 'since he disappeared immediately after the accident.'

'Disappeared?' My breath quickened. My head began to swim.

Greenwoode went on. 'Naturally, we wanted to speak to the stagehands at the end of the evening. Tom was responsible for hanging the chandelier and lighting the candles. When the audience had left, Mr Garrick attended to your father, and I rushed off to look for Tom. I searched everywhere for him in the theatre.' He spread his arms wide. 'He was nowhere to be found.'

'Does Mr Sancho know of this?' Belle asked.

'No!' said Garrick, abruptly. 'And I'd rather you didn't mention it to him for now. Until we're certain. I'm sure there's a perfectly reasonable explanation. Tom's a good lad. Troubled, maybe, but he's not . . . Look. I feel terrible.

Ignatius is a very dear friend. He is imploring me to restore *Othello* to the stage . . . The best thing I can do for him is to press on with making the theatre as safe as I can and start up our rehearsals again as soon as possible.'

He pushed himself up from the table with an air of finality.

'Speaking of which, if you don't mind, ladies . . .' he went on, opening the door and waving us out, 'we have a crew meeting in five.'

Do you ever get the feeling that adults are trying to get you out of the way so that they can get on with the 'real' conversation they want to have? It seemed to happen to me a lot. I tried not to let it bother me, though.

Belle and I headed straight to my father's dressing room. There, with Garrick and Greenwoode out of the way, we could have *our* real conversation too.

Chapter Eighteen

Papa's dressing room was a true cabinet of wonders, somewhere between a giant wardrobe and a miniature theatre. Glittering waistcoats, velvet breeches and silken stockings hung from rails like flat, lifeless body parts. On one wall, blank-faced wooden heads stared down from crooked shelves, each head wearing a wig or a carnival mask or, in some cases, both. Looking-glasses in every corner reflected the room over and over again. It was like being trapped inside a magnificent jewellery box.

Belle was pulling the writing desk from where it sat in the corner to the centre of the room.

'So it's important that we make notes as the enquiry progresses,' she was saying. 'We don't want to miss any important details. Let's try and find some order in the chaos.'

She sat down at the desk and laid down the leather pouch

she had brought with her. From it she produced an inkwell which she placed carefully on the desk and a small box, from which she took a newly sharpened quill. She whipped out a clean sheet of paper and fired up the quill. I marvelled inwardly at how prepared she was.

'Right!' she declared. 'So you talk it through Lizzie, and I'll write.'

I walked around the room to get my thoughts moving.

'Let's go back to the beginning,' I started. 'When you arrived at the theatre on opening night, a tall, hooded figure ran out in front of your carriage. You said you saw them go inside the theatre. By which door?'

'The stage door. I remember wondering whether they were part of the production . . .'

'Because the stage door's ordinarily just for cast and crew,' I agreed. 'And you said it was at five o'clock, which was before the doors opened to the public. So, if someone went through that door and they weren't a member of the theatre company, surely someone would notice?'

'Good point,' Belle said, writing hurriedly. 'And,' she added, 'they would need a key.'

'Then someone – possibly the same person – was hiding behind the curtain on the balcony above the stage. And in the moment after we both saw them, the chandelier fell to the stage, nearly crushing my father.' I sighed. He had come so horribly close to being seriously hurt. 'But *he* believes it was an accident, that the chandelier was too heavy.'

'As does Garrick, it seems,' said Belle.

'But Greenwoode thinks that it was Tom, the stagehand, who dropped the chandelier.'

Belle sat back and pondered for a moment. 'Do you think it was Tom we saw above the stage?'

I didn't, to be honest. But then, I had hardly seen

anything. Just a moving shape. And then a memory stirred – the night I got home late from Belle's . . .

'I can't be sure,' I said slowly, 'but – someone was watching the shop on Saturday night. After I got home from your house.'

Belle looked startled. 'What? Why didn't you say anything before?'

'Well . . . it was dark,' I said. 'By the time I got outside, they were gone. If they were ever there, that is.' I hated how uncertain I sounded.

'Trust your instincts, Lizzie. Maybe they're watching your father.'

I shook away the thought in my mind.

'How well do you know Tom?' asked Belle.

'Not very well . . .'

I tried to recall all the interactions I'd had with Tom. He practically flattened himself against the wall whenever we passed in the corridor. Tried to hide his height by hunching. Didn't seem comfortable with himself somehow.

'Does he have a motive?' Belle asked, quill poised.

'Not that I know of,' I said. 'But he did have opportunity, I suppose. Greenwoode said he was stationed above the stage for the performance AND that he disappeared afterwards.'

'So maybe he's our prime suspect right now?' said Belle. 'If we believe Greenwoode, that is.'

She moved a sheet of notes off to the side and started another.

'Look, Belle, there's something else . . .' I hesitated. 'In the Tower this morning, someone was there.'

'What?'

'She may have followed me up there. I don't know . . .'

'*She?*' Belle said sharply. 'It was a woman?'

'She said her name was Meg.'

Belle resumed writing. 'Go on . . .'

'She asked me what I was doing up there, whether I'd found anything. I didn't tell her about the address. I hid it in my pocket. But she warned me off. Told me to stop snooping around.'

Belle was writing furiously as I spoke.

'But – she told me her name,' I added. 'Why would she tell me her name if she was guilty? *And* she knew who I was. She mentioned my father. Almost as though they were friends.'

'So why would she want to harm him?'

'And if she did want to harm him, why would she speak to me and tell me her name?' I said. 'That doesn't make sense.'

'If your parents know her, maybe you could ask them about her?' Belle offered, dipping the quill in the ink with one hand and reaching for a third sheet of paper with the other.

I bristled.

Sometimes I believed my parents knew everybody in London. If we were out as a family, we could barely get from one end of the street to the other without bumping into a dozen friends or acquaintances along the way. I was secretly praying that Meg did *not* know my parents, or that if she did, she had no plans to mention our meeting.

Fact: if my mother caught one whiff of what we were up to, she would shut us down with a snap of her fingers.

There was another matter worrying away at me.

'Something bothered me about Garrick's manner,' I said. 'It felt like he was covering something up. And why was he so over the top about what a fantastic production it would be?'

I didn't want to ask Belle directly why Garrick had been so keen to make such a good impression on her, but that's what I was thinking. She must have guessed though, because she shifted awkwardly in her seat.

'Uncle William is one of the patrons of the theatre,' she said. 'He has invested money in the production. I suppose Garrick feels he owes him an explanation.'

So that was it. *'Money talks!'* Mama often said. *'If you want to know where the power is coming from, follow the money!'* I had no idea what it was like to wield that kind of power. A grown man acting as though he were almost afraid of Belle, afraid of what she might say about him.

'So we can't necessarily trust Garrick,' I said. 'He's

obviously not concerned about my father's safety, and he seemed to want to cover up for Tom.'

'What about Greenwoode?' asked Belle. 'The two of them clearly don't get along.'

Greenwoode was the first adult who actually seemed to believe that someone dropped the chandelier on purpose.

'He made much more sense to me,' I said.

'Perhaps. But he made me uneasy too. Though, of course,' said Belle, sitting back, 'we know that neither Garrick nor Greenwoode could have been on the balcony when the chandelier fell – because they were both on stage!'

That hadn't even occurred to me. Of course. Both Garrick and Greenwoode were on stage next to my father, just seconds after the chandelier had fallen. There was no way that either of them would have had enough time to get down from the Tower if they had been on the balcony. So that left us with Tom and Meg.

'Let's speak with Puck tomorrow,' I suggested. 'He's a friend. I trust him and he knows Tom better than I do. He might know where to find him. And we should try and find a Phoebe Street or a Phoenix Street. My mate Mercury could help us there.'

'Agreed,' said Belle. 'But we should be careful, Lizzie. If Tom is mixed up in this, maybe Puck is, too?'

'No way! Not a chance!'

Even I was surprised by the force that shook my voice.

Belle held up her hands as if to calm me down. 'If you say so. But from now on, we need to explore the theatre without being seen, without drawing attention to ourselves. We handled that Greenwoode and Garrick scenario rather clumsily. We need some kind of cover, so that we can interview people without letting on that we are investigating.

'Which brings me to my next point,' she announced, laying the quill on the table.

Something in the tone of her voice told me to pay attention.

'Don't go off on your own again like that, Lizzie. We don't know what we're dealing with here. It's dangerous.'

I struggled for an answer in my defence but found none. The truth of it was that I had been really afraid up there in the Tower.

'And correct me if I'm wrong,' Belle continued, 'but you and I – we're a team, aren't we?'

'Of course,' I said sheepishly.

'So from now on, we work together. Where one of us goes, so does the other. Deal?'

She thrust out her hand towards me. I took hold and we shook on it, hard and heartily. No curtsy required.

'Deal!'

CASE NOTES on
The Othello Case

- **Crime:** Attempted murder?
- **Intended victim:** Ignatius Sancho
- **Scene:** Stage balcony, Theatre Royal
- **Weapon:** Chandelier, dropped from a great height
- **Time and date:** Friday 11th April 1777, around 8 of the clock, evening

Prime suspect:
Tom Johnson, stagehand
- Tall, like the shadow seen on the balcony Friday 11th, and the figure spotted outside Sancho's shop on Saturday 12th
- Motive: unknown
- Opportunity: yes – stationed above stage for performance
- Responsible for chandelier on the night
- Disappeared immediately after the event (according to Greenwoode)

Secondary suspect:
Meg

- Who is she?
- Snooping around balcony on Monday morning
- Warned Lizzie away from crime scene, asked if she'd found anything
- May be known to Sancho family?
- Motive: unknown
- Opportunity: knows the Tower, has been there before?

Also questioned:
Garrick

- Theatre manager, actor, friend to Mr Sancho
- Very nervous, not keen to share information
- Keen to go ahead with production (even if not safe?)
- Protecting Tom
- On stage at the time of the crime

Greenwoode

- Assistant director, always at odds with Garrick
- Melancholic and intense by turns
- Seems concerned for Mr Sancho
- Believes it may have been attempted murder
- Suspects Tom
- On stage at the time of the crime

Chapter Nineteen

B elle and I had agreed to meet at the theatre the following day. First item on the agenda was to speak with Puck and find out from him as much as we could about Tom.

My worries had tumbled like dice round my head all night. I couldn't imagine that Tom had intended to harm my father, but I *could* believe that he had dropped the chandelier by accident, then run away. Seeing him in my mind's eye sidling past me along the wall, I could imagine exactly that. Was it him we had seen on the balcony perhaps, then?

Papa's spirits, however, were lifted high by Garrick's letter – 'Garrick says that rehearsals will resume almost immediately! That as soon as I am well enough, I should return to work. We must rise to the challenge like a phoenix from the ashes!'

So Papa would return as soon as he felt well enough? That could be a matter of days! What if we did not solve the crime in time? He would be in danger as soon as he set foot inside the theatre again!

To make matters worse, I was feeling a little uneasy about Belle. She seemed to want to run the investigation her way, and I felt like she was bossing me around. After all, it was *my* father we were trying to help!

Meanwhile, Mama had, rather infuriatingly, invited Belle round to supper that evening.

'But she's *my* friend!' I protested. 'Surely I should get to decide when she comes for dinner!'

'Of course!' said Frances. 'And by the time you get round to it, she could get here on ice skates . . .'

I turned to Mama for support. She was plucking a giant chicken. Small white feathers drifted in zigzags to the floor. It was only Tuesday – we never stewed a chicken on Tuesday!

'But Mama, what's the rush?' I pleaded.

'What's the delay?' she retorted, throwing her eyes back at me. 'You meeting Belle at the theatre again, you can come back here together in her carriage. Joshua says he'll bring you. And you better fix yourself up smart for supper!'

So Joshua was in on it, too. Perfect.

On the way to the theatre, I stopped by the office where the *Daily Advertiser* was printed. This was the last stop on

Mercury's pick-up round before he started his deliveries. I wanted to ask him about the address I had found.

Mr Weekes, the editor-in-chief, was shoving clothes into a bag and muttering to himself. His lank, brown hair was plastered to his forehead with sweat and his shirt was a good two sizes too small. He had the look of a beaver about him. When he heard the shop bell ring he froze and narrowed his small brown eyes at me.

'Whadda *you* want?' he snarled, looking me up and down.

I lifted my chin. Mercury had told me he didn't much care for Mr Weekes. Now I could see why.

'I'm looking for Mercury!' I tossed back. 'We've not had a delivery from him this past two days.'

'Well, when you find him, you can tell him from me he's out of a job!' said Mr Weekes. 'Unreliable little so-and-so. Upping and disappearing in the middle of the night! What about my deliveries? Go on, hop it, you! Skedaddle!'

Before I could say a word, he lurched towards me and pushed me out of the door.

'No wonder he left!' I shouted at the window as Weekes slammed a wooden shutter.

Maybe Mercury had gone to seek out another employer. It would not have surprised me in the slightest.

When Belle arrived at the theatre to meet me, she was breathless and excited.

'I've got it!' she said.

She pulled me into Papa's dressing room and shut the door firmly behind us. With a grand flourish she produced a series of printed newssheets and pamphlets and spread them out on Papa's writing desk.

Town and Country magazine, *Stage Door* . . . Not this again. Reading gossip columns was not going to help us solve this!

'If we want to interview the cast without raising their suspicions, *this* is how we do it!' Belle announced.

I sighed. 'Explain . . .'

'We pose as writers. Diarists of the theatre!' she said. 'We say that we're writing articles about life on the London stage, that sort of thing. That way we can find out exactly who thinks what about your father, about each other, about the production. We can source the information we need without anyone knowing that we're investigating a crime!'

'But I *know* some of the people here,' I pointed out. 'Puck, for example. He's my friend. He'll tell us what we need to know, I'm sure.'

'Of course. But he's one person with one perspective, Lizzie. We'll have to listen to a range of voices if we want to get the broader view.'

'But will they actually *talk* to us?' I'd been coming to the theatre with my father for weeks now and most of those actors had ignored me outright.

Belle waved away my concern with a little flutter of her hand. 'We'll put on a bit of a performance ourselves! We're keen journalists and fans to boot, intrigued to know more about these fascinating people and their world. We'll use flattery to draw them out. People love talking about themselves, about their work. If we ask the right questions, we could solve this mystery ourselves.'

Solve this mystery ourselves. Those were the words that pulled me in. If I wanted to make sure my father would not come to harm, we had to find out as quickly as possible who might want to harm him, and why. And *we* had to stop them.

I sighed. 'All right then, I suppose . . .'

'Wonderful! Come on, let's rehearse. You go first!'

'What?'

'Go on . . . just imagine I'm an actress and you want to interview me. How are you going to start the conversation?'

Oh, man. Role play. Nightmare.

'Erm . . . Miss Dido Belle, I'm Lizzie . . . I'd like to ask you some questions.'

I shrugged. This was silly. Belle nodded and rolled her hand around in the air, urging me to go on.

'Erm. Well, we're writing a piece for . . .'

'*Stage Door* magazine!'

'*Stage Door* magazine, and we wonder if . . . if . . . Oh, this is nonsense!' I resisted the urge to sweep the whole pile of silly magazines on to the floor. 'I'm not an actor, Belle. I'm me! I'm happy being me and I don't want to be anyone else!'

'Of *course* you can be you,' Belle said earnestly. 'Just be the you that wants answers to the questions. This time round, watch me. We'll start with . . .' She ran her finger down the cast list. 'William Ash! He plays Iago. He should know a thing or two about villainy!' she added, with glee.

'I hardly think we need to suspect the man that actually saved my father's life!'

'True,' Belle conceded. 'But we're trying to find out as much as we can about the people here, remember?'

'What about Puck? I thought we were going to speak to him about Tom?'

'We'll go to Puck straight afterwards, I promise.'

I wondered if Belle often used her charm to get her own way.

She carefully packed away her writing set and handed it over to me. 'I'll do the talking for this one. You can be the scribe.'

And with that she sashayed out of the door and up the corridor towards William Ash's dressing room.

As I went to close the door, I noticed a small paper envelope on the floor. How long had it been there? I looked up and down the corridor and saw only Belle's retreating figure.

I bent to pick it up. The front of the envelope was blank. On the back, a plain seal in red wax, no imprint. I pushed my finger underneath it and opened up the paper.

Inside, in a tight, even hand sloping to the right, were the words:

Little girls should be seen and not heard.

Stop asking questions if you know

what's good for you!

My stomach lurched.

'Come on! This is his dressing room!' called Belle as she reached the corner of the corridor.

I folded the paper carefully and slipped it into my pocket. I would not share it with Belle for now. No point putting her off while she was just getting into her stride.

Chapter Twenty

'Enter!'

Even though I knew that Mr Ash was Mr Ash and not Iago, and that he had saved my father's life, the sound of that sinewy voice set me on edge.

The room was sparse and spare: the only items of furniture were a small dressing table and a three-legged stool. Ash strode across the floor, one hand behind his back, the other brandishing a dog-eared copy of the script. He peered over his pince-nez glasses at us and sank into a deep bow with an elaborate sweep of his arm – as was the fashion.

'Mr Ash,' said Belle slowly, holding her skirts up above her ankles and curtsying dangerously low. 'Do please forgive the interruption. I am Dido Belle, and this, my dear friend and colleague Miss Elizabeth Sancho.'

I wasn't going to curtsy. But I gave a solemn nod, serious

enough to be construed as a half-bow, I thought.

'Charmed, I'm sure,' returned Ash. 'And to what, may I ask, do I owe the pleasure?'

I stepped forward. 'First of all, I want to say thank you! For saving my father's life . . .'

'Dear, dear girl,' he said, his eyes misting up. 'For a dear friend, anything. A terrible affair, indeed. He is well, I trust?'

I nodded. 'He wants to come back to the theatre, but –'

'Mr Ash!' Belle interrupted. 'We do not wish to take up too much of your time, but Miss Elizabeth and I are currently engaged in a writing project. A – distraction, shall we say – after the stresses of recent events. A project to celebrate the illustrious contemporary practitioners of the theatre!'

Come again? She sounded like Papa!

Ash beamed and brought a lace-edged handkerchief to his face to conceal a coy smile. 'Well, of course . . .'

Belle continued. 'Would you do us the honour of featuring in an article we are composing for *Stage Door* magazine? A celebration of the creative contributions of the great actors of the age to this production of *Othello*?'

'My dear girls!' gasped Ash. 'You are shining a light on the most refined of the arts – that of theatrical performance. You are to be commended! Please, sit down, and I will tell you all!'

Belle flashed a side-eyed smile at me and waved me

towards the chair and dressing table. 'Miss Sancho, if you will?'

On cue, I sat down, took out the writing materials and got ready to make notes.

'Mr Ash,' Belle began. 'You are an experienced character actor, playing Iago. Can you tell us more about your role as the villain of the piece?'

Ash beamed. 'Indeed I can, Miss Belle! As you will know, when the play begins, Othello is married to Desdemona, a young woman whose father opposes the marriage. They are very much in love, but the other soldiers find it hard to believe that Desdemona has chosen him. Othello has a colleague in the army. Someone he confides in . . . Iago.'

He paused, letting the name hover over us menacingly for a moment.

'Iago is jealous of Othello's success, but he hopes that Othello will promote him to be his lieutenant. When Othello promotes a wealthier young man called Cassio instead, Iago is enraged! He is slowly consumed by a quiet, slow-burning, bitter hatred and vows to destroy Othello's career, his marriage, and his life!'

What a snake! I thought, with a shudder.

'He sounds horrible!' said Belle. 'Why does Othello trust him?'

'Well . . .' Mr Ash considered for a moment. 'Iago is

very good at making people believe what he wants them to believe. *I am not what I am!* He plays with words to secure people's trust. He claims to be honest, but he spins endless lies.'

I put the quill down. 'But why?'

'Why indeed, Miss Sancho!' Ash spread his arms wide. 'Motive! Motive! Motive! What drives any one of us to do the things we do? What drives a man to destroy another man? Why does Iago loathe Othello so? And why does he engineer his destruction?'

He put the script down and brought his fingertips to his forehead, closing his eyes for a moment, lost, it seemed, in thought.

'What drives people to hate?' he murmured.

He looked up suddenly, and said wildly, 'The green-eyed monster! You see, Iago is consumed with envy. He is envious of Cassio, whom Othello promotes over him. And he is envious of Othello. Iago is jealous of Othello's military success, of his popularity. It drives him to distraction that Othello is loved by Desdemona. Understanding this, for me, is key to understanding my role.'

I listened, spellbound.

'What does it mean to be Iago?' Ash continued. 'To be so consumed with self-loathing, to turn that hatred out towards another. He takes that jealousy and he crafts it into a weapon. When he lays his trap for Othello, and leads him to believe that Desdemona has been unfaithful with Cassio, Othello in turn will be consumed with jealousy and with rage.'

Tragedy was intense, that was for sure.

'Mr Ash,' said Belle. 'Please could you tell us more about your working relationship with your fellow actors? Mr Sancho, for example?'

'Ah, Ignatius! An admirable fellow indeed. If he is well enough to return, he will be the first African to play Othello on our great stage. It is an honour to share that sacred space with a wordsmith such as he! Alas, still, he is recovering from the shock of the cursed chandelier.'

'You think it was cursed?' I asked, quill hovering mid-air.

'Forgive me, a mere turn of phrase,' said Ash. 'Though who can say? The stage is a strange and mysterious place. Who knows what shadows haunt its corridors, what ghosts are concealed beneath the boards?'

I raised my eyebrows at Belle.

'It was a shocking incident,' Belle said gravely, sincerely. 'It must have been very . . . upsetting for you all . . .'

Here, she eyed the actor carefully.

Ash's face lit up in agreement. 'Well, quite. Though of course, there is an even more sinister aspect. You see, if we do open again, all the extra publicity means that we'll probably be looking at a sell-out run! And if the play makes more money – well, we *all* make more money!'

I put the quill down. 'Excuse me?'

Ash waved a hand. 'It's like when there was a scandal over at the Bristol Playhouse concerning their leading lady when they staged *The Rivals*. Her reputation was in ruins! Everyone was worried that the show would close altogether. But all the publicity worked wonders for the show. Audiences flocked to it in their thousands. It's very possible we might be looking at a similar situation. Front page news and all that.'

Belle and I exchanged glances.

'I see,' said Belle. 'Well, thank you so much, Mr Ash. You've been most – instructive!' She beamed and extended her hand, dropped from the wrist. He took it in his and gave another of those floor-scraping bows. 'We've got everything down and we'll be sure to send you a copy just as soon as we go to print!'

'What did you think?' said Belle once we were out in the corridor. 'Did you get down everything he said?'

Well, not exactly everything.

'I got the gist of it,' I said. 'Jealousy and lies. And the fact that everyone might stand to profit from a terrible accident. That puts just about everyone in the frame!'

'Well, we'll just need to keep asking around,' said Belle. 'The important thing is that we have a record of what everyone has said.'

'Can we go and see Puck now please?' I asked. I was tired of keeping up this pretence. I was glad not to be an actor!

Puck was at work in a room on the east corridor where the costumes were kept. I knocked and we entered.

He was standing in front of a looking glass, talking to his reflection, dressed in a blue greatcoat that was far too large for him. The sleeves draped comically past his hands, giving his arms a monstrous look. The trousers hung in bags all the way to his ankles. He slashed at the air in wide swathes with a sword and lunged like a fencer, pushing the sharpened steel through an invisible opponent.

'If that thou be'st a devil, I cannot kill thee!' he roared.

We watched him with curiosity for a moment. He caught sight of us in the looking glass, spun around, aghast, and skittered behind a wooden changing screen decorated with crimson roses.

'Don't you knock?' came the voice from behind the screen. High, fluting, not yet dropped to the pitch of a man's.

'I did knock!' I said, rolling my eyes at Belle as we wandered around the room. In one corner was a rail of greatcoats, edged with silver, studded with gold buttons. In another, an array of dresses, elaborately adorned with laces, frills, ribbons and bows. Belle took a seat beneath the window while we waited.

'You're supposed to knock and wait!' Puck complained, emerging from behind the screen in a plain fustian shirt and breeches.

He was skinny. Agile and lithe-limbed, like a dancer. His straight jet-black hair was swept back from his face. When he spoke, his large, dark eyes shimmered with mischief, but I had also seen them hold a deep sadness. Puck was dear to me. I trusted him.

'Hey, Puck,' I said with a grin.

'Hey, Lizzie,' Puck returned. 'How is your papa?'

'On the mend, thank you. Bouncing back with a vengeance, in fact.'

'And who's this?' Puck was staring at Belle, a little too doe-eyed for my liking.

'Puck, Belle. Belle, Puck,' I said. 'Look, Puck, we're here to ask you about the incident with the chandelier.'

A strange silence fell over the room like a cloud passing over the sun.

'Oh. That,' Puck whispered, staring at the floor.

'My papa wants to join rehearsals again as soon as he is well enough,' I said. 'But I'm worried . . . I'm not sure the theatre is safe for him.'

Belle stepped forward. 'We were wondering if you could tell us your version of events that night, please.'

Puck frowned. 'You don't think that I had anything to do with it, do you?'

'No, of course not,' Belle said, laying her hand on his arm. Puck visibly melted a little. Seeming not to notice, Belle went on. 'We're just trying to piece together what may have happened. You see, we think we saw someone. Above the stage. And we're wondering if it may have been . . . Tom?'

Puck's eyes widened. 'Above the stage? On the balcony?'

'Yes,' said Belle.

Puck looked puzzled. He got up and walked over to the window, stared out as if trying to arrange his thoughts. Then he spun back to us and shook his head. 'That doesn't make sense.'

'Why not?' I said.

'Well, on opening night, Tom was responsible for the chandelier, and I was supposed to be helping with costume changes. We usually meet in here before a performance for something to eat. Miss Lamont brought us some soup that night.'

'Miss Lamont?' The name was familiar.

'Susanna Lamont,' Puck said. 'She plays Emilia in the play. She's so kind. Garrick says she spoils us rotten.' He looked coy for a moment. 'She dropped off some vegetable broth for us and I waited for Tom. But he didn't turn up. I waited and waited. I went off round the theatre to look for him but I couldn't find him anywhere. And I had to start work. The actors were calling for their costumes.'

'Did you tell Garrick or Greenwoode?' Belle asked, seating herself at the window.

'No. I was worried that Tom might get into trouble,' Puck confessed. 'I didn't want him to lose his job. I thought I could cover for him. I even went up to the balcony to light the chandelier myself, but the door to the Tower was locked. Tom has the only spare key. I figured maybe he hadn't come in to work at all. So I didn't say anything to anyone. I just went back to the wings and carried on with my own work. But then, when the chandelier fell . . .'

He looked up at me, his face stricken. 'I really am so sorry, Lizzie. I just don't know how it happened! I was really frightened, so I ran round to Tom's house. I knocked and knocked – I don't even know whether I expected to find him there. He didn't open the door, but he called out to me. I remember thinking his voice sounded – odd. He said that he was sick. That I should go away and let him rest. He said he'd come and find me when he was feeling well enough. So . . . so I left.'

'And you haven't seen him since?'

Puck shook his head. 'And I didn't want Garrick and Greenwoode to blame him for the chandelier. If he had been where he was supposed to be – or at least sent word ahead so that I could have been up there – the accident might never have happened!'

He sat down in the window-seat beside Belle and pulled his knees up to his chest. 'I feel terrible. Tom is like a brother to me. He's always looked out for me. If it weren't for him, I wouldn't even be here.'

'How do you mean?' Belle asked gently.

Puck rubbed his nose with the back of his hand. 'Been in London since I was seven, I have. Got here all on my own.' He nodded at me. 'Lizzie knows. I grew up in Calcutta. My mother died young from sickness. Got no brothers, no sisters. So I decided to come to London to look for my father. He was a sailor. A lascar for the East India Company. Posted in London in between voyages. He said that wherever he went, the Company would look after him. Pay him well. That's what he believed. I just wanted to find him. Stowed away on a spice ship, all the way from Calcutta. Imagine that!'

He nudged Belle with his elbow. 'Weeks at sea. Tucked myself into a storage room below decks, creeping out at night to snatch what bread and water I could from the sailors' rations. I was relieved when they found me! The captain took pity on me. Said he would keep me on board if I could entertain his crew. I sang pretty well and knew how to tumble . . . We docked at Tilbury. Off I went on my own again, to find my father. But no chance. No one had heard his name, and no one wanted to help me.'

He looked miserable at the memory of it.

'I was begging for pennies in Covent Garden when Tom found me. He was a carpenter at the theatre and said there was work to be had, said that he would put in a good word for me with Mr Garrick. That's how I joined the company.

Sometimes I get to sing and dance in the cast, but most of the time I work backstage. But there's good pennies in it and a safe place to sleep at night. I'll never forget what Tom did for me.'

Puck looked up at me. 'Whoever dropped the chandelier that night, I don't believe for a moment it was Tom.'

My thoughts were whirling. If what Puck was saying was true, Tom might not have even been at the theatre that night!

'Right,' I said, jumping down from the dressing table. 'Let's go!'

Belle looked at Puck and back to me. 'Where to?'

'To see Tom of course. Maybe he can shed some light. Puck – you lead the way!'

ACT III

Outside, the sky was a blank space. The cold, white light of midday seared my eyes after the gloom of the theatre.

We crossed Bow Street and headed towards Covent Garden.

As we made our way west through the market, stray dogs scampered and sniffed around the fruit and vegetable stalls, their ribs showing through their skin, hoping to snuffle away any fallen scraps of food. Children darted in and out of the crowds, running errands for extra pennies to buy some bread, some soup, an apple.

We stopped at Molly Parson's bakery and bought four vegetable pies – one for each of us and one for Tom. Molly wrapped them up in a cloth for us. 'Keep them nice and warm,' she said, her cheeks flushed from the fierce heat of the oven.

'This will cheer him up!' said Puck, his eyes lighting up at the thought of seeing his friend again. He crossed Long Acre and strode ahead of us up King Street. 'This way!' he called over his shoulder. 'Tom lives at St Giles. Over at the Rookery, with the other Blackbirds.'

'Blackbirds?' asked Belle. She was struggling to keep up, not used to negotiating the chaotic walking traffic in this part of the city.

'*You* know,' I said, taking her arm to steer her out of the way of an oncoming coach. 'The Blackbirds of St Giles?'

She shook her head. It struck me how much I learned from our family conversations at dinner, and I wondered how it must be for her, to be the only Black person living in her house.

Puck hung back for a moment to allow us to catch up.

I pointed up the road ahead. 'From here to Gower Street and over to Oxford Street is the parish of St Giles. My mother says that the people who live here are some of the poorest in the city. Some of them have escaped enslavement, some were free born. But many don't have money to live on and they can't get work. They're known as the Blackbirds.'

We turned into Broad Street. Here, the streets narrowed, and the wooden houses leaned over the roads towards one another, as if for support. Taverns stood at every corner. The poverty was tangible. The streets were filled with people whose faces were pinched and drawn with hunger, whose clothes hung off them in tatters.

Puck disappeared into a side alley. I pulled Belle towards the narrow gap between a sow-gelder's and a blacksmith's. As we squeezed through, it opened out again into a long alleyway. At the end of the alleyway was a wooden fence. Puck crept his fingers across the wood until he found a loose plank. He hit it with the heel of his hand and it gave way.

'This way!' he called, holding it open and ushering us through.

On the other side was a maze of crooked buildings. Broken windows gaped from soot-covered walls.

'Not many people know this way,' Puck confided. 'It's a secret back entrance to Phoenix Street!'

'Phoenix Street!' I stopped dead in the road. Since I'd had no luck finding Mercury, I'd forgotten all about the address in my pocket. I fished it out and showed it to Belle. 'Belle, you don't think . . .'

'It must be!'

We were whispering; neither of us wanted to alarm Puck.

'Here's where Tom stays,' Puck was saying proudly, as we came to a narrow black door. Number 21.

Belle and I exchanged glances. So whoever had been in

the Tower had had a note of Tom's address.

Puck knocked briskly. 'I hope he's feeling better. He'll know what to do. You'll like him.'

Silence. He knocked again.

'Tom! It's me, Pu—!'

'Ssshh!' I shook my head at Puck and put my finger to my lips. The last thing we needed right then was to draw attention to ourselves.

Belle peered in at a small window, holding her hands on either side of her face for a better view. 'I can't see anything,' she whispered. 'The curtain's drawn across the window . . .'

I kept my eyes fixed on the entrance to the alleyway behind us.

Puck tried the door. It pushed open with a creak that made me shiver, even in the pale grey light of the afternoon. Tentatively, one behind the other, the three of us stepped inside. It seemed colder in the house than it was outside. The room was cloaked in a sickly gloom and a stale smoky smell filled our nostrils.

'Tom?' ventured Puck, in a small voice.

I slipped over to the window and pulled away a tattered piece of cloth that had been strung up to block out the light. A cloud of dust escaped and swirled in the air for a brief moment before settling slowly to the floor. The weak light revealed a small, dank chamber. In one corner, a narrow pallet bed, the coverlet pulled neatly across it. In another, a wooden workbench where several planks of wood, a hammer and a saw lay, all covered in a fine layer of dust.

There was no sign of life.

'What's that smell?' said Belle, wrinkling her nose. 'The fire?'

I crossed to the hearth and crouched down, holding my hand out over the ashes.

'They're cold,' I said, looking around the room. 'The fire's been out for days.'

'What *is* that smell?' insisted Belle.

'Tobacco,' I murmured, remembering the smell in the Tower.

'But Tom doesn't smoke,' said Puck, miserably, sitting down on the empty bed. 'Where is he? I don't understand. He was too unwell to move just a few days ago! Where could he have gone?'

It was obvious that no one had been living here for days.

'Is there anyone he might have gone to stay with?' Belle offered hesitantly. 'Family perhaps?'

Puck shook his head. 'He doesn't have anyone any more. He calls me his little brother, but we're just very close friends.'

Next to the bed was a small chest of drawers. Puck opened them one by one. Inside were two shirts, two pairs of breeches, a hair comb, a drinking mug and a set of keys.

'Tom doesn't have much, but what he does have is still here. And these are the keys to the theatre.' He fished them out and held them in his lap.

I sat down on the bed next to Puck.

He turned to me suddenly, his eyes wide with alarm. 'What if he was really *really* ill, Lizzie? There's cholera and consumption in these streets! What if . . . ?'

The possibility that Tom was dead entered the room and lingered like an unwanted guest.

No one spoke.

It was me who finally broke the silence.

'I think we need to let someone know that he's missing, Puck.'

Puck sighed. 'I'll tell Miss Lamont,' he conceded finally. 'She looks out for us. And she knows a lot of people. She'll help us.'

I cast my eye once more around the room, taking in Tom's meagre furniture and scant possessions. Had we missed something, some clue or sign that Tom might have left as to what had happened to him or where he might be? But the room remained stubbornly silent, resolutely empty.

'It doesn't feel safe here,' said Belle quietly, a faint tremor in her voice. 'I think . . . I think we should get back to the theatre.'

Outside, the sun struggled to pierce the clouds. As we emerged from the alleyway, people hollered and guffawed around us in the streets, their banter weaving an odd counterpoint to our anxiety for Tom.

An elderly Black man sat propped up in a doorway. On his head, he wore a tri-cornered hat bedecked with a ship, masted, its white sails dirty and tattered. His left leg was a wooden post below the knee, and a crutch lay at his side. His blue coat was frayed around the edges and the buttons, once silver and shiny, were now dulled and worn down with age. He stared at the ground in front of him. His lips moved but no sound came from them.

I took from my pocket the vegetable pie I had bought for Tom. It was still warm in my hands but was cooling fast. I held it out towards the old sailor.

'Sir, if you please . . .'

The man looked up with rheumy and unfocused eyes. He nodded his thanks as he took the pie from me with a shaking hand. He gazed upon it as though it were a jewel mined from the depths of the earth. His eyes flashed with hunger. As I ran to catch up with the others, a cracked voice followed me up the alleyway in broken notes of song.

'When the pie was opened, the birds began to sing!
Wasn't that a dainty dish to set before the king!'

When we arrived back at the theatre, a young woman in a magenta taffeta dress and an ostrich feather in her hair was just stepping into the street from the stage door. To her chest she clasped a tiny brown-and-white King Charles spaniel, its fluffy ears flapping as it wriggled around in her arms.

'Miss Lamont!' Puck cried, and ran across the street to greet her, sending a horse-drawn coach skittering over to the side of the road. The driver hurled a curse over his shoulder and whipped the horses back into action.

'Puck, dearest, you must take more care!' Miss Lamont said, drawing her to him and ruffling his hair.

He gave a gentle smile, sheepish, bashful.

She looked at us appraisingly. 'And who, might I ask, are your *charming* friends?'

Her voice sang with mischief.

Puck turned and waved us towards her with a flourish of his slender hand. 'My good friends – Miss Elizabeth Sancho and Miss Dido Belle! Or, to their friends, Lizzie and Belle!'

'Lizzie and Belle!' Miss Lamont exclaimed. A bright sound, like champagne glasses clinking. 'Charmed, I'm sure!'

Puck sighed. 'I need to talk to you, Miss Lamont – urgently. It's about Tom.'

She frowned, alarmed, put a hand to her chest. 'Tom! What's happened? Is he all right?'

Puck hesitated. 'I think he may be . . .' he cast a glance my way, 'missing . . .'

'Missing?' gasped Miss Lamont. 'Oh, dear child, do come inside quickly and tell me all! Girls, I'm glad to have met you, but I really must attend to this . . .'

She put her arm around Puck's shoulder and led him inside.

I wanted to follow, but Joshua was waiting across the street, sitting a-perch Belle's coach. He nodded when he saw us. Of course! Dinner.

I shouted after Puck, 'We'll come back tomorrow!'

'Absolutely!' he called over his shoulder. 'I'll report back!'

In the privacy of the carriage, left alone once more with Belle, I was uncertain of what to say. It was a shock realising that the address I had found was Tom's, and even more of a shock finding Tom's place empty. Why had Tom disappeared and where had he gone?

Belle was looking over the case notes. 'Lizzie, show me the address again.'

I produced it from my pocket and handed it over.

'So whoever was up there that night had Tom's address written down,' said Belle. 'Why?'

I shrugged. I was still concerned that perhaps he was our culprit after all, and I wanted time alone with Papa to ask him about Tom. Did they get on? Had he noticed anything unusual about him recently? But how was that going to happen this evening?

Belle put the notes down in her lap and looked out of the window. 'Maybe they were after the keys to the theatre? To the Tower perhaps? Puck said that Tom had the only key.'

'No, he said that Tom had the only *spare* set. But Tom's keys were still at his house . . .'

'I wonder if this address is what that woman at the Tower, Meg, was looking for,' Belle said, putting it into the pouch along with the case notes. 'If it is, she won't be happy that you've found it.'

When the carriage pulled up at home, Papa came out to greet us.

'Joshua, my dear fellow, are you sure you will not join us for supper? Mrs Sancho has acquired some premium chicken from Hertfordshire and some of the finest peppers to have recently landed this way from Barbados!'

'Very kind of you, Mr Sancho,' said Joshua, tipping his hat. His voice was rich, soft and sonorous. I realised in that moment that I had hardly ever heard him speak. 'But I have an appointment with my brothers and sisters at the Guinea Coffee House. I shall return for Miss Dido Belle at eight o'clock precisely.'

Papa nodded and shook Joshua's hand. 'Very well. I quite understand. Another time, perhaps. We have much to discuss, I am certain.'

With that he placed his fist over his heart. Joshua reciprocated. I did not understand the gesture, but knew that I had just witnessed something important; a show of solidarity, perhaps.

I helped Belle down from the carriage and showed her inside. Now that Belle was seeing my home for the first time, my stomach felt fluttery. What would she make of our three-roomed house? Kenwood it was not. As we crossed the threshold, the smoky aroma of chicken pepper stew enveloped us, and quelled my fears more than a little.

Perhaps Mama's cooking was all I needed.

'Ignatius! Is that Belle arriving?' chimed Mama from the back room.

Er . . . and me?

Mama emerged from the kitchen next door, taking off her apron and hanging it up on the wall. When she saw Belle, she burst into smiles and rushed towards her, arms flung wide. 'Belle, dear girl! Welcome, welcome, welcome!'

Mama grabbed Belle in a rapturous hug.

'We have been so excited to see you my dear! Do come in and sit down, please! Come and meet the Sancho family!'

She ushered Belle into the kitchen-cum-dining room. Over the hearth hung a huge steaming cast-iron pot: the source of the heavenly chicken fragrance.

'Mmm! Thyme? Cayenne? Onion?' asked Belle.

My mother beamed like a summer morning in spring. 'Why yes! How did you know? You eat like this at home?'

'Aunt Betty is a keen collector of herbs and spices,' said Belle. 'Sometimes we stroll together in the kitchen garden and gather herbs for dinner. I've learned to spot a few plants by their scent alone. But nothing I've eaten at home has smelled quite as delicious as this!'

Mama looked positively girlish. I had not seen my mother act this way before. Not since the boxer Bill Richmond had visited the shop, in any case. Everyone in the family remembered *that* day.

'Well, let's hope it tastes as good as it smells,' she purred, patting her hair anxiously. 'Do sit down, girls. Belle, where would you like to sit?'

'Come sit here by me,' piped up Mary. 'I hear you have a harpsichord at Kenwood. Do tell me what you like to play! Perhaps we could duet later!'

Frances looked as though she were ready to box Mary's ears. 'In that case, I'll sit here,' she said brusquely, moving Billy's little bowl one space up to make room for herself on Belle's other side.

Seeing Belle sitting between my sisters, I was shot through with a sudden pang of envy. Everyone seemed to be making a terrible fuss over her. The chair opposite Belle was empty. I pulled it out noisily and dropped into it without a word, feeling utterly invisible.

Mama and Papa took their places at each end of the table, and the little ones sat either side of me: Billy by our father, and Kitty by our mother.

Mama ladled out the steaming stew – a rich broth of chicken, yam, tomatoes and onions, flavoured with thyme, cayenne, onion and chilli pepper. A side dish of okra – 'For strong blood!' Mama insisted.

'Belle, pass your dish and let me serve you – no, Billy, guests are served first!'

'Kitty, don't hit your brother . . .'

'Pass the bread down!'

'Pass the bread down, *please*! Where are your manners?'

'Where's the water? Whose job was it to get the water for the table?'

'Mary! Did you forget the water?'

'I'll get it!'

'Billy, close your mouth to eat, darling. No, *after* the spoonful has gone in – Frances, fetch a cloth too, please!'

I glanced over at Belle. I'd never really seen my family through someone else's eyes before. What must she think? Suddenly we seemed all noise and mess and chaos and – well, lack of refinement.

I didn't usually care a jot for manners. So why was I so concerned right now?

Chapter Twenty-Four

24

As everyone settled into the business of eating, the only sound to be heard was the scraping of spoons on bowls.

It was my father who spoke first.

'Belle, we must confess, we have been following your uncle's work closely since the Somerset ruling in '72. It had quite an impact on our community.'

'What's the Sunnyset ruling?' asked Kitty, elbows in the air as she made great efforts to cut her yam into tiny pieces the way she liked it.

I was glad she had asked so that I hadn't had to. Belle looked from my mother to my father as though waiting for one of them to answer.

'I'm sure you could shed as much light as we could, Belle,' said Mama. 'In fact, it would do us good to hear your opinion on it.'

She gestured towards Belle to encourage her to speak, as she so often did with us. 'Other people will speak for you if you give them the chance,' she would say. 'But how will you know if they are telling your story in the way you wish it told? You must take every opportunity to speak the world as you see it.'

Belle dabbed at the corners of her mouth with her napkin and placed it with care on the table. All Sancho family eyes were on her. Even the little ones were paying close attention. She cleared her throat.

'It's a law that my uncle passed a few years ago,' she said. 'It's named after a man called James Somerset. He was an African man who had been "purchased" and enslaved by a man called Charles Stewart in America. Stewart brought Somerset to England. While they were here, Somerset escaped. Stewart paid men to go and re-capture Somerset. They threw him in chains and kept him imprisoned on a ship in a dock by the Thames. The ship was bound for Jamaica.'

We had all fallen completely silent as we listened with intent.

'Stewart meant to take Somerset back into enslavement and put him to work on a plantation. Some people heard Somerset's cries and contacted the authorities. Somerset knew what fate awaited him, and appealed to the courts.

Granville Sharp, an Englishman opposed to slavery, offered to represent Somerset.'

Belle became more animated as she narrated Somerset's history.

'There had been several cases that brought to light the status of African people who had previously been enslaved. The law was uncertain. The big question was, if someone ran away from their so-called master, could they be forced back into enslavement? People were being sent back to the sugar plantations, to work under the lash . . .'

'Where they have little chance of living more than a few years, so brutal are the conditions under which they labour!' added Papa.

'Ignatius,' Mama said in that strong-soft way she had. 'Belle was speaking. Belle, go on.'

Belle nodded. 'Uncle found it very difficult to make the ruling. Lots of people were putting enormous pressure on him to rule in favour of Stewart.'

'Well, they would!' interjected Frances. 'They don't want Britain to abolish slavery because of all the money they earn from it!'

'Quite,' concurred Belle. 'If Uncle ruled that Somerset should go free, people might interpret it as a sign that no one could be kept enslaved here.'

'Which is exactly what happened, no?' asked Frances,

topping up Belle's glass of water.

'Eventually, yes,' said Belle. 'Granville Sharp and a young lawyer named Francis Savage made a strong case. And Somerset himself had gone to great lengths to bring the case to court. But not many people talk about that.'

Mary chimed in: 'So, thanks to Somerset's bravery, Granville Sharp's persistence and Mansfield's final decision, it is now illegal for someone to capture a person of African descent on the streets of Britain and send them to the

Caribbean in enslavement.'

I suddenly had the sense that perhaps I had not listened carefully enough to certain dinnertime conversations. In this moment, I wished I had.

'We celebrated in style,' said Mama wistfully. 'The Dog and Duck was full of rejoicing that night! Punch and wine and dancing till dawn! Even the children stayed up late with us. For a brief moment, we all felt as though we were free.'

'But you – we – *are* free!' cried Belle, looking around the table.

Her words fell into an uncomfortable silence.

'Until all our African brothers and sisters are free, Belle,' said my mother in a low voice, holding Belle with her eyes, 'we are none of us really free.'

She stood to clear away the dishes, paused at the table. 'The trade in enslaved people still persists, girls. Hundreds of thousands of our sisters and brothers today are working for no wages on plantations in the Caribbean and in America. We must keep pushing hard towards abolition and emancipation. Ignatius has worked very hard for this family –'

'As have you, my dearest –' murmured Papa, reaching for her hand.

'And we count ourselves very fortunate,' Mama continued. 'The girls are learning music, they read and write. And we run our own business. But how many of our brothers and sisters in Britain can say that right now? What are we able to imagine collectively for our children? What opportunities can we hope for, for them? Until everyone is able to imagine the best for their children – the best opportunities, the best choices for their future – we are none of us free.'

The fire crackled in the hearth while we considered Mama's words.

'A truly edifying speech, dear heart,' said Papa, getting up and lifting the heavy pot back to the stove. 'And we must represent ourselves at every level of culture. Until the lions have their own storytellers, the story of the hunt will always glorify the hunter. That is why I must return to the stage.'

He spread his arms wide. 'And now – perhaps some music to round off the evening?'

After everyone had helped to wash the pots after dinner, Mary took her place at the harpsichord and invited Belle to join her in a duet. Then Frances brought out a pile of books and asked Belle for her opinion on their arguments. She had heard about Lord Mansfield's famous library and was still angling for a visit. Kitty and Billy were enamoured of the soft silk of Belle's dress, and every time she stood up, they took great delight in hiding among its folds and clinging to her legs.

Papa disappeared to the back room to rehearse his lines.

I felt utterly lost. Even Belle looked like she was more at home than me. Defeated, I climbed the stairs to the bedroom and curled up on the bed. I would probably not even be missed.

Footsteps on the stairs.

'Belle?' I said, sitting up.

Mama.

I turned back to the wall, wiping tears of frustration from my face.

'It's good to meet your friend, Lizzie,' said Mama, sitting on the end of the bed. She was rubbing coconut oil into her hands to soften them after the day's work.

'So I see,' I muttered into the pillow.

'You wanted us to meet her, didn't you?'

'Yes, but . . .'

'But?'

'But it's as though now she's here, she's hardly noticed me.' I sat up, keeping my eyes in my lap, pulling at a loose thread on the sheet. 'It's as though . . . as though, all of a sudden, she belongs to everyone else.'

'Well, I suppose she does in a way,' said Mama. 'She is our friend because she is your friend. But that doesn't make her any less yours. Surely you can see that her making such an effort with us is her way of showing her friendship for you?'

'It's just the last couple of days . . . I don't know,' I muttered. 'Everything's suddenly going wrong! And I'm so worried about Papa.'

'Don't you worry about your father. He's tougher than you think,' Mama reassured me. 'He's been through worse than this. But you and Belle have spent so much time together . . . you must be getting along well, no?'

'In a way,' I admitted. 'But our lives are so different. The way people look at us when we're together . . . And the way people behave around Belle . . . even our family. Even . . . even you!'

I wasn't making much sense through my sobs, but Mama grabbed me and wrapped me up in her arms in one of those super-tight hugs that you couldn't escape even if you wanted to. The kind that said, *'No matter what you are feeling right now, no matter how angry you are, no matter what you say, you are my daughter, and I will always love you with all my heart.'*

'We're making her welcome Lizzie,' she said. 'She's obviously important to you. Your sisters showing respect for that. We showing respect for that. What you want us to do?'

I didn't have a reply.

'I don't expect she has many friends of her own living in that big house up on the Heath,' Mama went on, spreading out her fingers and inspecting her nails. 'No mother of her own . . .'

My mother had this amazing knack of starting the thought she wanted you to finish.

I remembered that day when I first visited Belle. 'I've never met another Black girl before,' she had said. I remembered that she had not seen her own mother since she was Kitty's age. I remembered how alone she had looked as she climbed the steps back into that big, empty house. Suddenly my own feelings of envy and self-pity seemed mean-spirited.

As though reading my mind, Mama said, 'You can hang on to those dark thoughts you holding right now, or you can open your heart a little and let them fly.'

I drew in a long breath and let out a longer one.

'What was I thinking?' I groaned. 'What will she think of me?'

From outside the bedroom window came the sounds of voices in the street. I dashed over and looked out just in time to see Belle climbing into the carriage. A guilty feeling sank like a stone to the pit of my stomach and lodged there.

Papa was standing on the pavement talking to Joshua and handing him a leather pouch. My father's skills as a writer of letters meant that people sometimes asked him to write letters on their behalf. Was he doing such a favour for Joshua, perhaps?

As the carriage drew away, I thought to myself how strange it was the way that our feelings could colour the way we viewed a situation, could change our perception of things. Difficult feelings about a friend might even, for a time, make them appear an enemy. And yet this was just a contortion of the truth, brought on by our emotions. As though a coloured filter had been placed over our view of someone, so that no matter what they did or said, we saw it in the light of the orange emotion or the blue emotion we were experiencing in that moment.

Maybe the mark of true friendship was its ability to withstand the whole spectrum of feelings. Maybe it was not just how you behaved towards one another when you were feeling the sunrise colours that counted; when you were bathed in the rosy glow of early friendship – but how you treated each other when sunshine yellow turned green, when green drifted in to blue, when blue sank into indigo, when indigo bled into a deep, painful violet.

Chapter Twenty-Six

26

When I opened my eyes the next morning, the residue of my guilt clung to me stubbornly like the smell of bonfire smoke. I knew that I should have made an effort to speak to Belle before she returned home. I knew that I should have tried to make peace between us, or at least have been more honest about the thoughts I had been having.

But part of me needed time away from Belle for a while, and I was glad of the prospect of spending a day at the theatre on my own to focus on the investigation. What else could I uncover about Tom, or Meg?

Everyone knew Belle, or wanted to know her. On my own, I had a better chance of being – well, invisible. Maybe I could scope out the theatre unseen, remain hidden and watch comings and goings, eavesdrop undetected on conversations.

When I came down to breakfast, Papa was spooning out tea leaves from the large glass jars into paper bags for sale. Mama stood at the stove, stirring the day's porridge. Kitty and Billy were sitting on the floor, rolling a wooden ball towards one another. At one of the tea tables in the shop, Mary and Frances sat poring over a magazine.

On the kitchen table lay the day's newspapers.

The Daily Advertiser

Ruthless youth flees scene of crime

The Bow Street Runners are looking for a boy by the name of Tom, following allegations of attempted murder at the Theatre Royal, Drury Lane. The youth, who worked at the theatre as a carpenter and stagehand, dropped a vast iron chandelier on to the stage during the theatre's stellar opening night performance of William Shakespeare's *Othello*. Witnesses say they saw the tall, dark youth running through the streets shortly after the incident, which left would-be star Ignatius Sancho concussed and confused.

Opinions within the theatre company are divided, with assistant director Dominic Greenwoode still fearful for Mr Sancho's life, while director and theatre manager David Garrick is keen to press ahead with the show.

Mr Greenwoode told us, 'Our priority must be the safety of our actors. An attempt has clearly been made on Sancho's life. He should not return until we can guarantee his safety.'

Meanwhile Mr Garrick, keen to dismiss claims of a blatant disregard for the safety of his colleagues, said:

'We have taken serious measures to ensure the safety of the theatre and of our cast and crew. Do not be alarmed by recent events. We look forward to welcoming the crowds a week on Saturday to what is set to be the most exciting theatrical production of the year!'

One of the show's female stars, Susanna Lamont, who said she thought of the boy as an adopted son, put out this pitiful plea for his return: 'Tom, please come back to the theatre. Accidents happen. Be brave: come back and face the music. We miss you.'

'Garrick and Greenwoode at odds again!' scoffed Mama from the stove. The air was heavy with cinnamon and apple-infused sweetness. 'Those men can't agree on anything. They really think Tom try to kill you, Ignatius?'

'Of course not, dear heart. Greenwoode's overthinking things as usual. Accidents happen. Tom's a gentle soul. He's probably terrified. Especially now the Bow Street Runners are involved.' Papa pushed the jars back on to the shelf and took his black periwig from where it sat on the headstand. He arranged it carefully over his own hair and straightened his jacket.

'I don't know if we'll see him at the theatre again,' he said. 'If he knows what's good for him, he'll stay away. It's just the press whipping things up, no doubt. Tom's not someone to fear, that's for certain.'

'So you're going back to the theatre then, Papa?' I asked, afraid of the reply.

'Indeed I am!' he cried, scooping Billy up into the air. Billy threw his head back, gurgling and giggling uncontrollably. He looked like a tiny version of Papa.

'Careful, Ignatius,' warned Mama without turning away from the stove. 'You want to put your back out before you even get up on the stage again?'

Papa set Billy down and spun Mama around to face him.

'Dear heart! Think of the impact of this performance! An African takes to the stage – a lead role, played by a brother. It feels more important now than ever for us to be visible, to be seen! Who knows what could come next? Think of the roles I could write for others!'

'True, Ignatius – up to a point.'

Mama pushed him gently away from her and turned back to stirring the porridge. Papa and I exchanged glances. Whenever Mama said, 'Up to a point,' we knew that she was about to challenge.

'What I mean is – what are they seeing when they see Othello?' Mama said. 'It's still a sticky question for me. The way the play end just not right, Ignatius. A man so driven to desperation by jealousy he take his own wife's life? That the way we want them to see us? That the story we want to be telling on stage?'

Was that how the play was going to end? With Othello murdering Desdemona? That was too horrible to think about!

Papa looked forlorn for a moment. 'One step at a time, dear heart. One step at a time.'

'If something need changing, it need changing, Ignatius. No point going half-half on this now.'

'I hear you, my dearest. Let me give it some thought.'

Papa wrapped Mama up in his arms and planted a gentle kiss on her left cheek.

I cleared my throat.

'Lizzie!' Papa cried, unperturbed, disengaging himself from Mama and offering me his arm. 'Would you do your father the honour of accompanying him to the theatre today?'

Chapter Twenty-Seven

The day was wreathed in a soft light, the city cloaked in a fine mist. We turned out of Charles Street and strolled towards Westminster Abbey. Papa loved this route, as it took us past St Margaret's Church, where he and Mama had married one freezing winter.

'I remember it as though it were this very morning, Lizzie. The trees were garlanded with snow and a peaceful hush settled on the city. As though the world were holding its breath while we said our vows. That, Lizzie dear,' Papa said, patting my hand on his arm, 'was the beginning of the greatest happiness I have ever known.'

'Papa,' I said, 'Why does the play end that way?'

He turned me to face him. Then he pulled out the handkerchief I had given him and held it up to the sun. The flames seemed to wink in the daylight. His voice, when he spoke, was low and heavy.

'Iago asks his wife to steal Desdemona's handkerchief, so that he can plant it on Cassio. Then he tricks Othello into believing that Desdemona has given Cassio the handkerchief as a token of love. He convinces Othello that she has been unfaithful. The sight of the handkerchief in Cassio's hands is "proof" that sends Othello into a downward spiral of jealousy and propels him into a murderous rage.'

He clasped the handkerchief to his chest.

I swallowed hard. Was this how Papa's role on stage would end? I couldn't bear the thought of it.

'I've always found that difficult, Lizzie,' he continued. 'The only role available to us on the stage right now is a man so driven to distraction by his own unbridled jealousy that he murders his wife. That is the tragedy. But what if there were some way to change it? To transform it? To give Othello back his humanity?'

'So why don't you just do what Mama says and change it?' I asked.

Papa nodded. 'Indeed, I shall think on it. This could be the beginning of something momentous, Lizzie. We need to write our own plays, our own roles. To write characters that tell all our stories. Our tragedies, yes, but our comedies too. Our joys, our magic, our family lives. Stories penned by us about our loves, our passions, our talents, our challenges and our dreams. Think, Lizzie, what a wonder that would be. The written word gives us voice, not just now but in the future. Empowers us to speak to those not yet born. Imagine, Lizzie! Imagine!'

I thought of that day in Belle's library. All those books, but where were people like Belle and me on the printed page? Papa was right. If we wanted to see ourselves on stage, in books, in poetry, we had to write those stories ourselves.

From the abbey we headed south to walk by the river. The hazy white sunlight painted wavering ribbons of light on the surface of the Thames and a salty scent drifted on the air, blown upriver from the sea. Gulls careened in wide circles over our heads, scanning the mud beaches for scraps of food or smaller birds to snatch up into their curved beaks. Men shouted to one another as they rolled hogshead barrels up and down gangplanks or emptied nets bursting with jumping silver fish into wooden vats. Small fishing boats rocked gently against one another in the jetties that reached out from the docks.

Masted ships crowded the waterline, their sails flapping, beaten by the breeze.

We paused a moment to look out over the water.

My father sighed.

'For some, Lizzie, the sight of a ship brings hope.

It signals the possibilities of journeys: of new horizons, new lands, new life. Where will this vessel take me? Who will I become when I get there?'

His words hovered with me for a moment, then seemed to fly away from us on the wind.

'Not so for all, dear child,' he said quietly. 'As you know, for me, and for so many others, ships stir up dark memories. While the trade in people continues to haunt our ports, our hold on the life we live in this city is precarious. Even now, after the Somerset ruling, people are snatched from our streets and forced on to ships bound for the sugar plantations of the West Indies. There, stripped of their name, the life they knew, their very humanity, they toil all day under the hot sun, under the lash. Danger awaits us around every corner. We must take care, Lizzie.'

Papa lifted my chin and spoke gravely.

'Promise me you will watch your step, precious child.'

I nodded. How could I explain to him that in my mind, *he* was the one in danger? *He* was the one who needed protecting?

A large sloop drifted past us like a ghost boat, momentarily blocking the sun and casting a shadow over us both before it surged on downriver.

Right now, making my father safe and returning him to his rightful place on the stage seemed more important than ever. I squeezed his arm tightly and we walked on together through the bubbling, bustling throng of the city we both called home.

Chapter Twenty-Eight

I promised Papa that I would stay either inside or close to the theatre all day. He kissed my forehead and retired to his dressing room to prepare to go on stage.

As soon as he was out of sight, I slipped down the corridor to the stage door. If Tom did decide to return, I wanted to be the first to know it. The door was locked – there was no key in the keyhole with which to let myself out. This meant I had to go back through the auditorium, through the lobby and out of the front entrance. From there I made my way round to Russell Street, to keep an eye on the stage door from across the road.

I hid myself in the shade of a narrow doorway, a perfect place from which to watch the comings and goings behind the theatre. The street bustled with people passing to and fro, largely taking no notice of me. Sometimes there were advantages to being virtually invisible. On this occasion,

I was glad not to be seen.

For the first hour, nothing.

The door remained stubbornly closed. No activity to report.

A delivery girl arrived with a basket of oranges, round and glistening. My mouth watered at the sight of them. She knocked loudly on the stage door. It opened slowly, the person behind it obscured from my view by the door itself. The girl laughed at something they said and handed them the basket. The door closed once more.

Another half-hour passed.

And then, I sensed a shifting in the atmosphere. A darkening.

I think I felt their presence before I saw them. A creeping sensation, as a shadow passed over me.

A giant man stalked by and crossed the street to the theatre. He wore the long black leather coat of a highwayman, caped about the shoulders, the high collar turned up and buttoned to the top, so that his face was masked and only his eyes were visible. On his head he wore a black tri-cornered hat tilted low over his brow.

It was, without doubt, the shadowy figure from the balcony.

My heart wedged in my throat.

I pressed myself into the doorway.

The Shadow stopped at the stage door and turned to look over his shoulder, as if to make sure no one was watching.

What if he had returned to attack my father again?

I sprinted into the road, straight into the path of two horses pulling a cart of vegetables. One reared back on its hind legs with a whinnying scream, eyeing me wildly. The driver spat curses, frantically pulling on the reins to control the agitated creature as the cart toppled over and potatoes and cabbages rolled all over the road. I stuttered an apology and darted across the street – just as the Shadow slipped inside and pulled the door shut firmly behind him. I grabbed the handle. Locked!

What about the front entrance? Could I head him off at Papa's door?

I shot around the edge of the colonnade, burst into the lobby and tore down the corridor to Papa's dressing room. I threw open the door and scanned the room. His chair was empty. No one here. I raced down the corridor towards the stage door. No one there!

Where had the Shadow disappeared to? And where was Papa?

The sounds of the actors' voices floated towards me. I crept up to the curtain at the back of the stage and peeked through. The rehearsal was in full swing. I watched the silhouetted actors from behind: they moved like walking shadows. There was Mr Ash, and there was Papa!

Thank goodness!

In front of them, row upon row of empty seats in the auditorium.

And now Mr Ash was hissing at the invisible audience:

'As he shall smile, Othello shall go mad;

'And his unbookish jealousy must construe poor Cassio's smiles, gestures and light behaviour quite in the wrong.'

For a moment I lost myself in the performance, relieved and intrigued to see my father on stage.

Waiting in the wings, half in shadow, was Mary Robinson, the woman who played Desdemona. Papa, I knew, liked her dearly; Mama humphed loudly whenever her name was mentioned. Beside her, Puck looked on, open-mouthed, spellbound.

Garrick sat in the front row of the stalls, watching intently, nodding, making notes on a sheaf of papers in his lap.

There was a bang behind me. The stage door!

I flew back and opened it just in time to see the tall, caped figure stride purposefully up the street, eastwards towards Aldwych. The early swirls of afternoon fog were settling on the city. I stepped outside into the chill air and gave chase, walking at speed, following at a safe distance. The black boots kept on walking, the figure passing in and out of sight through the crowds, in the thickening fog.

The minute he turned a corner I sprinted up the cobbles after him. He marched on to Fleet Street. I kept up my pursuit. He leaned forward into his gait, almost falling into his own deliberate steps. Why was he going east? Was he headed towards St Paul's? If I followed him to his final destination, would I find Tom?

He paused outside a jeweller's and gazed in at the window. I pressed myself into a doorway, no more than ten yards behind him. When I peered out, he was facing me head on. There, staring with the flat black eyes of a shark.

I froze. Dread spilled through my veins, chilling my blood.

Was this the person who had warned us in writing to leave off the investigation?

He pulled a steely, knowing smile, then swiftly turned and marched up the street ahead. It were as though he expected me to follow.

I quickened my pace, keen not to lose him in the crowd. Suddenly, off to my right, I saw another familiar face pushing through the throng of people. Meg! She was heading fast towards the Shadow. She must have felt my eyes on her because she turned and caught my gaze. She frowned at me, shook her head – a warning? – and pushed on through the crowd.

So this time I had caught *her*! On her way to meet her accomplice, it seemed!

They both moved so quickly, and I wove in and out of the crowds, desperately trying to keep eyes on both of them as I pushed on through the sea of bodies. Arms and elbows and bags and shawls all pressed against me as I struggled to keep moving forward. By the time I burst out of the crowd, the street ahead was empty. I looked around. Neither the Shadow nor Meg were anywhere to be seen.

I could not believe I had lost them. I knew with dead certainty that the man I had been following was the man I had seen above the stage. And outside the shop. And if that were true, then he was the person who had tried to kill my father. He had been just within my grasp, and I had lost him.

And Meg too! Had they been at the theatre together? Had she let him in? And where had they gone to now? Perhaps a meeting to discuss their next steps? She was clearly an accomplice.

Exhausted and bitterly disappointed with my failure, I turned back towards the theatre and bumped hard into someone walking straight towards me. I tumbled backwards on to the pavement, grazing my elbow as I fell.

'Oh, goodness gracious, I'm sorry!' said the woman, reaching out a hand to help me up.

It was Susanna Lamont.

Chapter Twenty-Nine

'M y dear girl, are you quite all right?'

Susanna Lamont took my hand and hauled me on to my feet. The dog under her arm was all a quiver, shaken no doubt by the impact of our collision. I shrugged myself into a more composed state and nodded, wiping the dirt from my breeches.

'Yes, yes, I'm fine, thanks . . .'

I glanced over my shoulder, hoping to catch a glimpse of Meg or her accomplice somewhere in the moving crowds. But it was no good. I could not see their faces among the many that milled and thronged around us. There was nothing for it. They had got away from me.

'Lizzie, isn't it?' Miss Lamont said, with a disarming smile. 'Do you need to sit down? Could I offer you a cup of tea, perhaps?'

She waved a gloved hand vaguely in the direction of the Jamaica Coffee House across the street.

'No, no, it's all right, thanks.' How could I have let them escape me? They were right here!

'Are you quite sure? You took quite a tumble!' She smiled warmly, hesitated a moment, then said, 'Forgive me for asking, Lizzie, but I've just come from the theatre. Won't your father be wondering where you are? The rehearsal finished half an hour ago –'

No!

Without another word I waved a hasty goodbye and sprinted up Fleet Street towards the theatre. When I arrived, Papa was standing under the colonnade with a face like thunder.

'Lizzie! Where on earth have you been?' he scolded. 'I've been waiting an age for you!'

I mumbled my apologies as we crossed the piazza, said something about needing to get some air.

'And after my warning to you this morning! Perhaps you would rather spend your days in your room if you cannot be trusted about the town!'

As the sun disappeared into the murky waters of the Thames, and the navy night spread through the city, we walked home in silence.

Back home in the shop, we found a strained atmosphere.

The musicians were sitting in silence at their usual table. Will was staring into the bottom of his tankard. George was watching the fire with fierce intent, the leaping flames reflected in the pupils of his dark eyes. Mary and Frances were slumped into an armchair, leaning on each other as though for comfort. The room was tight with tension.

Mama moved quickly from table to table, paying intense attention to the task of clearing away the cups and plates that littered them. As we entered, she took off her apron and rushed towards us, clasping us both to her in a tight embrace.

'Oh darlings, darlings, I'm so glad you're home!' She stepped back and wiped her eyes. 'Lizzie, my sweet, go upstairs please. There's a letter in your room from Belle. I need to speak with your father.'

But Mary and Frances were here! Why shouldn't I stay too?

'I'd like to stay and listen,' I said, pulling a chair back from the nearest table.

'Lizzie.' My mother's voice dropped nearly an octave. 'Did you hear me ask you to go upstairs just now?'

'Whatever it is, I think I'm old enough to hear it –'

'I said go!' she said sharply, her eyes flashing.

I stamped up the stairs, seething. Why did everyone think I was too young to hear what was happening around me? If only they knew just how much I had learned! Things they didn't seem to have any idea about.

When I reached the landing, I hesitated. Whatever Mama was going to say, I felt I had a right to hear it. I retraced my footsteps back down the stairs, taking care to avoid the floorboard that creaked. Halfway down I stopped and crouched down. I held my breath and pressed my ear to the cool wall to pick up what snatches of conversation I could.

The dampened murmur of their voices was punctuated with the clatter of crockery.

'. . . missing since Monday . . .'

'It must be him again . . .'

'We'll need to speak to the sons and daughters . . .'

'. . . call a meeting . . .'

Who were they talking about? Who was missing? I strained to catch a name, but the swift tap of footsteps approaching the tea-room door sent me scampering up the steps and into my room.

There, on the bed, lay an envelope, addressed to me. I opened the letter and a great wave of relief washed over me when I found a page of writing in Belle's precise, elegant hand.

Dear Lizzie,

I do sincerely hope that all is well with you?

I must apologise for leaving so suddenly the other evening. I ventured upstairs to bid you goodbye, but you were deep in conversation with your mother and I did not wish to disturb you.

I hope you will excuse me taking the liberty of sharing my thoughts with you. My uncle and aunt each have their own preoccupations, and my days stretch out before me, full of quiet and solitude, with little chance for conversation.

Uncle William grows increasingly irritable. Some aspect of his work is clearly bothering him. Aunt Betty says that in spite of the Somerset ruling, people of African descent still face danger of kidnap on the streets of London. This is giving Uncle serious cause for concern.

I realise I have, perhaps, been rather naïve. I have underestimated the dangers that so many people face in their day-to-day lives.

I have been continuing with the investigation as best I can here at home and have some news to share.

Both Garrick and Greenwoode visited Uncle yesterday – but separately, which I found rather odd. Garrick arrived at breakfast time. I offered to take in tea, so that I might hear some of the men's conversation. Garrick was clearly flustered, and at pains to persuade Uncle not to withdraw his support for the production. He kept insisting that 'Sancho must take to the stage!'

After Garrick had gone, Greenwoode arrived, a little after lunch. He told Uncle that he was concerned for your father, worried that there was perhaps some kind of plot on his life. He said he had shared his concerns with Garrick, but that Garrick had brushed them aside. He added that it was 'almost as if Garrick did not care for Sancho at all.' Uncle, rather characteristically, heard them both out, but did not give away his own thoughts on the matter.

Meanwhile I have been scouring the newspapers daily for any clues that might help us and have updated our case notes with some intriguing information.

Do come when you can, so that I may share this with you. Know that you are always welcome.

Your friend, in hope,
Belle

Oh, Belle! Had she heard all the things I had said to Mama that night? What must she think of me? And yet she had had the courage to write to me. And she was still pursuing the investigation! I resolved to visit her early the next morning. I had news of my own to share.

That starless night I shivered in my bed and was denied the privilege of sleep. Whether that was down to the merciless pinch of the night cold on my fingers and toes, the harrowing memory of the day's events or a stark fear of what lay ahead, I could not tell. But all I could see whenever I closed my eyes were those black shark eyes staring back at me: cold, hungry, remorseless.

Chapter Thirty

30

The following morning I rose early. I left a note for Mama explaining that I had gone to Kenwood to apologise to my friend. Mama would not be happy, but I simply had to go. I reassured her that I would ask Joshua to drive me home and that I would be home before dark. I hoped that this would be enough to fend off further questioning.

I decided to pass by the offices of the *Daily Advertiser* in case Mercury had gone back to work. If someone in our community really had disappeared, Mercury would know about it. But the office was closed, the door padlocked with a heavy iron chain. I peered in at the window. The printing presses stood motionless. There was no sign of Weekes or anyone at all. I would return tomorrow.

The walk to Kenwood was brisk and refreshing. The clean air of the Heath cleared my head of the dank fog of the city and helped to wake my brain after my sleepless night. The uphill climb was easier than I'd found it before, and thanks to my breeches I didn't have to worry about a silly dress dragging in the mud.

It was Belle who answered the door this time. Had she seen me approaching from her window? We both stood, awkwardly, for a moment, before anyone spoke.

I knew what I needed to do.

'Belle – I've come to apologise.' I toed the ground as if trying to kick away the traces of my embarrassment. 'I behaved like a baby the other night. I'm so sorry.'

She lowered her eyes. 'I'm sorry, too. I've been feeling awful. I really didn't mean to upset you. I was just so excited to meet your family. And . . . well, I've not really spent time with other people my own age before.'

There was a brief moment of silence while I tried to work out what to say next. 'Well,' I said at last. 'We could pick up from where we left off, perhaps . . .'

She smiled broadly, clearly relieved. 'Of course! It's what I've been hoping for.' She looked sheepish. 'I've been working on the investigation.'

'Yes! I got your letter!' I said. 'I think I've made some headway too, but . . . a lot has happened . . .'

'Come. I have something to show you,' she said confidentially, stepping outside and closing the door behind her.

She led me away from the house and up a hill towards a small, white outhouse. She dug around in her pocket for a key.

'The dairy!' she announced, unlocking the door and flinging it open. 'Aunt Betty sometimes entertains guests here for afternoon tea, but we won't be disturbed in here this week.'

The windowed walls flooded the room with sunshine. Around the edges of the room teetered pile after pile of books, newspapers and magazines.

'Uncle has most of the daily newspapers delivered and we have a subscription to all manner of magazines,' explained Belle. 'I've been comparing articles about the accident at the theatre. And I've been reading up about the history of the Theatre Royal.'

On a long trestle table were spread countless sheets of paper: drawings of the theatre and maps of the surrounding streets, notes on personality and character, and lists of questions.

'I've developed a system!' she said, with a mixture of pride and shyness. 'I thought, how can I work on the investigation if I'm not at the theatre? Background research! Here are my notes on location, for example. I've made some drawings of the theatre space showing the dressing rooms, corridors, the Tower, et cetera. Then I've made a map of the streets around the theatre to help us work out exactly where the culprit is going, how they might have made their escape, and so on.'

I peered closely at the intricately detailed street maps

Belle had drawn, showing Covent Garden, St Giles, the Strand: each road carefully labelled.

She pulled another pile of paper out of a folder. 'I'm keeping notes on each suspect in turn, adding to them whenever we learn something new. Noting down what they say, what they do, what others say about them, that kind of thing. And then I've used what Mr Ash told us: to start thinking in more detail about motive. I've been reading more Shakespeare tragedies to help with that!'

It was, it had to be said, an impressive piece of work.

'How long did this take you?' I asked in awe, looking over a list of examples taken from Old Bailey records of attempted assassination by falling object.

She waved her hand dismissively. 'I've been working on and off since that first night at the theatre. It helps me to see it all laid out like this.'

Looking at all the case notes made me realise I had to come clean about running into trouble once more without her.

'Belle, listen,' I said. 'Yesterday my father returned to work. I had to go with him. I thought that if Tom had seen the newspaper article he might decide to come back, tell us what he knows. So I scoped out the stage door during the rehearsals. And I saw the Shadow from the balcony. It's definitely not Tom. He's older, a huge man, in a long coat with a cape. I followed him –'

'Lizzie! What were you thinking?'

'What choice did I have? I couldn't let my father go to the theatre alone! And I thought that Tom might come back. So I set up watch by the stage door. And the Shadow just appeared. He went straight into the theatre. Either he has a key, or somebody let him in.'

I explained how I had given chase in case he meant to harm my father. I told her all about how I had followed him through the streets and how Meg had appeared once more; how they were clearly working together.

'Hold on. How do you know?'

'She was right behind him,' I said. 'I think they were going to meet somewhere. And remember, the first time I saw her, she was trying to clear evidence from the scene of the crime. *And* she warned me off.'

'It's a possibility, I suppose,' said Belle, casting her eyes upwards as though she were imagining the possibility right there and then. 'But,' she added briskly, 'we can't be certain. And we don't want to make any wrong assumptions.'

There was an expert tenor in her voice now, I noticed.

She looked hard at me. 'Did they see you?'

I realised that I had not been as careful as I could have been.

'Both of them did,' I admitted.

She nodded pensively. 'So where did they go?'

I slumped into a chair beside the table and shrugged,

feeling cross with myself. 'I lost them. I bumped into Susanna Lamont and they got away.'

Belle rubbed her temples for a moment, then jumped up and ran to the small mantelpiece on the far side of the room. There in a row stood a series of tiny china figurines. She selected four and brought them to the table. One by one she set them carefully down in a row.

'Right, so imagine the middle of this desk is the street. Here is the theatre,' she said, placing a book at one end. 'At the point at which you lose him, where is the Shadow?'

'Here,' I said, pointing to the other end of the desk.

Belle pushed down a miniature man in a purple Venetian carnival mask. 'So you are directly behind him, chasing, yes?' she asked, setting down a singing boy.

I giggled. 'Yes!'

'And Meg is behind you?' At this, she placed a sailor in third place, behind me. 'And then finally, Susanna Lamont.' A princess lifting the hem of her dress to show off her dainty ankles.

'Exactly.'

'Right,' Belle said, looking at the row of figures. '*You're* following the Shadow. And you think that Meg is on her way to meet with him. But what if *Meg* is following *you*?'

This definitely made sense.

'So you think she was trying to warn me off again?' I said.

'Possibly . . .'

I remembered the note I had picked up at the theatre. *Little girls should be seen and not heard. Stop asking questions if you know what's good for you.* It was still tucked away in my inside pocket. I toyed for a second with the idea of sharing it with Belle. Better not. I was certain she would call off the investigation if she felt we were in real danger.

She was still scrutinising the figures. Those tiny painted porcelain dolls that had looked so innocent on the mantelpiece now took on a more sinister air as we re-imagined their possibilities.

'What about Miss Lamont?' Belle asked, frowning. 'She was the last in the line?'

'Yes. I bumped straight into her when I turned around.'

'So she could have been following any one of you.'

'True! But Puck trusts her,' I mused. 'And she put an appeal in the paper for Tom to come home.'

'That reminds me!' cried Belle, jumping up and taking a magazine from a pile on the floor. *Town and Country.* Customers sometimes brought copies to the shop, and I had seen Mary reading it on occasion since it carried listings of upcoming dances and musical events.

Belle opened it to a double page spread and tapped it with her finger.

SUSANNA LAMONT AND MARY ROBINSON:
The True Rivals of the Theatre World by Peregrine Ponsomby

Well, readers, you've heard of *The Rivals*, the scintillating, sparkling theatrical comedy by Richard Sheridan. Now meet theatre's true rivals, Susanna Lamont and Mary Robinson!

Both tipped for the award of London's Leading Lady of the Year, Miss Lamont and Miss Robinson have been battling it out over lead roles in theatrical productions for many months now. It was Miss Lamont who took the role of Juliet to Mr Lewis's Romeo earlier this year. But it was Miss Robinson who pipped her rival to the post in auditions this week to play Desdemona in David Garrick's highly anticipated production of *Othello*.

Mr Garrick commended both audition performances, saying, 'It was a very difficult decision to make. There is no doubt that Desdemona is the more significant role – but two very talented actresses will grace our stage in the spring, alongside the exceptional Mr Sancho as Othello and Mr Ash as Iago.'

Both actresses have impressive followings among their fans, and with the award going to a public vote this year, there are whispers of the award becoming more of a popularity contest than a genuine appraisal of skill or technique.

When asked about the history of their feud, both Miss Lamont and Miss Robinson declined to comment.

'Let's speak to them both tomorrow,' said Belle firmly. 'They clearly don't get along. We'll tell them it's an interview for *Stage Door* magazine!' She looked up at me. 'If . . . that's all right with you?'

I wasn't keen, but as Belle was clearly making an effort to take my feelings into account, I thought that I should make an effort too.

'I'll have a go,' I said. 'Maybe you take the lead, though.'

'Great!' said Belle. 'So we present ourselves as correspondents for *Stage Door* – just like we did with Mr Ash! Only this time, we say we'd like to write a piece about women on the stage in the Golden Age of Theatre! Let's see what they are willing to reveal about each other and about the rest of the cast and crew. Right!'

She stood up decisively and disappeared into the small kitchen space at the back of the outhouse.

'I hope you like scones!' she called brightly. 'I made us tea!'

A few moments later, she returned, carrying a tray set with a pot of tea, two cups and a plate of scones. I cleared away our notes to make room. Belle set the tray down on the table and we spent the next half hour giggling through mouthfuls of tea and scone as we rehearsed our interview techniques as theatre correspondents.

The golden carriage clock on the mantelpiece chimed

four times, reminding me I had to get back before dusk. As we strolled back to the house, a gentle breeze shook the trees around us: a calming, soothing sound. At the front door, Belle rang to ask if Joshua could drive me home.

My new friend was fortunate in ways I could never understand, but it was clear she was lonely. Getting to know her was revealing to me just how lucky I was to have my family around me. And that I could afford to share them.

As the sky over Kenwood softened into evening, I felt a pang of sadness.

'I hope I haven't put you off visiting my family, Belle,' I said. 'We'd love to have you over again. Maybe that evening I just missed it being the two of us. Belle and Lizzie.'

'Lizzie and Belle!' chimed Belle.

The sounds of our names danced together in the air for a moment. This time, when she flashed that sparkling smile at me, I noticed how full of love and warmth it was.

CASE NOTES for
The Othello Case

- **Crime:** Attempted murder?
- **Intended victim:** Ignatius Sancho
- **Scene:** Stage balcony, Theatre Royal
- **Weapon:** Chandelier, dropped from a great height
- **Time and date:** Friday 11th April 1777, around 8 of the clock, evening

Prime suspect:
The Shadow – As yet unnamed. Tall man, broad-shouldered, wears black caped coat, smells of tobacco.

Sightings:
Friday 11th April
- A minute or so before 5 o'clock in road by stage door
- At around 8 o'clock, on balcony above stage

Saturday 12th April
- At around 8 o'clock, outside Sancho's shop

Wednesday 16th April

- At around half past 1 at theatre, suspect entered by stage door (has key?)
- After an hour or so in theatre (where? with whom??) suspect left by stage door and proceeded east towards Fleet Street
- Suspect turned and faced Lizzie, then disappeared into crowd

Secondary suspect:
Meg – Who is she?

Sightings:
Monday 14th April

- Snooping around theatre balcony in morning
- Warned Lizzie away from crime scene, asked if she'd found anything

Wednesday 16th April
On Fleet Street

- Travelling to meeting with Shadow?
- Following Lizzie?
- May be known to Sancho family?
- Motive: unknown

Also questioned:

Garrick

- Theatre manager, actor, friend to Mr Sancho
- Very nervous, not keen to share information
- Keen to go ahead with production (even if not safe?)
- Protecting Tom
- On stage at time of crime
- Visited Uncle to ask him to keep backing production

Greenwoode

- Assistant director, always at odds with Garrick
- Melancholic and intense by turns
- Seems concerned for Mr Sancho
- Believes it may have been attempted murder
- Suspects Tom
- On stage at the time of the crime
- Visited Uncle to ask him to cancel the production

Ash

- Saved Mr Sancho's life (unlikely suspect)
- Spoke of motive
- Mentioned possible financial gain for all due to publicity

MISSING

~~Tom Johnson, stagehand~~
- ~~Tall, like the Shadow seen on balcony Friday 11th, and the figure spotted outside Sancho's shop on Saturday 12th.~~
- ~~Was responsible for chandelier on the night~~
- ~~Disappeared immediately after event (according to Greenwoode)~~
- ~~Motive: unknown~~

Tom last 'heard' at home by Puck, through door, on evening of Friday 11th April, after chandelier had fallen.

Possible that Tom was **never at theatre** that night.

Someone (Shadow from balcony? Meg?) had **his address**, dropped it in Tower.

- Who wrote it down? Was someone sent to Tom's house?
- Tom's keys to theatre still in his room.
- Where is Tom now??

Chapter Thirty-One

We hovered outside Mary Robinson's door, wondering how best to approach her. According to some editions of *Town and Country*, she had a reputation for being difficult.

I knocked boldly.

'Come!' cooed a liquid voice.

I opened the door and peered in. The room looked like a Versailles boudoir. A rainbow of dresses stood to attention along the walls: an army of invisible women. Flowers shouted colour from every corner: crimson roses, purple peonies, golden daffodils, creamy white lilies. Their honeyed perfumes languished in the air. Boxes of chocolates lay open on the dressing table, their scarlet ribbons undone in indecent haste.

On the far side of the room, in front of a large looking

glass, sat Mary Robinson, swan-like. At her feet, next to the dressing-table, a large, grey, shaggy-haired dog was sleeping. Mary looked younger than she did on stage. There was a healthy energy about her, as though she had just run across a field and had arrived with you slightly breathless, but excited and full of vigour. Without make-up her skin was clear and fresh, and her hair hung loose about her shoulders in tangled rivers of chestnut brown. She turned to face us, her hazel eyes dancing with mischief.

'Well, I never!' she exclaimed. 'Look at you two! Gorgeous! Come in, girls and make yourselves at home. The more, the merrier!'

She swung back to the looking glass and turned her face this way and that, admiring her reflection. On the dressing table, a hairbrush, various pots of face paint and a well-thumbed copy of *Oroonoko*, by Aphra Behn.

'So what can I do for you, girls?' Mary asked, brushing her hair out so that it fell in full fluffy waves around her face.

Belle began. 'Well, Miss Robinson, we're very excited about the upcoming production of *Othello* –'

'And so am I! Been on tenterhooks, I have, this week, wondering if we're going ahead. Talking about keeping us in suspense . . .'

'And we'd like to interview you for *Stage Door* magazine.

We're running a piece on *Leading Ladies of the London Stage*, and we'd like to ask you about your experiences as a high-profile actress.'

Belle sounded so professional, so natural. How did she *do* that?

Mary Robinson skewered Belle with a sharp look. '*Stage Door* magazine?' She raised her eyebrows and turned to me. 'You two, doing an interview – with me?'

The idea had clearly ruffled her. Why?

'That's right,' Belle replied coolly. She unpacked her leather pouch, spread out her papers on the writing desk by the wall and prepared her quill with ink.

I watched the actress carefully as her eyes flickered over the writing materials. She stared archly as Belle headed up her page with the name 'Mary Robinson' and the date.

'Well,' Miss Robinson said finally, giving her shoulders a little wriggle in the looking glass. 'I don't mind if I do. Especially if it's women what's asking. That *Town and Country*'s always looking to stitch us up, if you ask me. You say one thing, and they print another. Might as well have been speaking into the wind! Go on then,' she said, dipping her fingers into a pot of alabaster and smoothing the thick white paint on to her cheeks in small circles. 'Ask away!'

I felt a shiver of guilt at the thought of deceiving her.

'Perhaps you could begin by telling us a little about your

performance as Desdemona?' Belle purred.

'Ah, yes! Desdemona! Intelligent, beautiful, honest, true. You could say it's typecasting! She's a good wife to Othello. Adores him.' At this, Miss Robinson threw a cheeky smile my way. 'That play don't do her justice, you know. Iago telling all them lies about her. And that Emilia don't help. Stealing Desdemona's handkerchief just 'cos her husband asks her to. She has a lot to answer for, that's for certain!'

'You think Emilia's to blame for Desdemona's downfall?' said Belle.

'Well, she certainly puts her oar in! Where's her sense of sisterhood?' remarked Mary. 'Take you two. I bet you look out for each other.'

We were trying to, that was for sure.

The young actress leaned over to me and whispered, 'I've heard you've been hanging about here more and more these days. You want to watch yourselves, though. Proper dangerous, I'd say.'

'Do you think so?' I asked, flashing a quick glance at Belle. What did Mary know?

'Falling chandeliers and the like! That's attempted murder, that is!'

What! She thought so, too?

'You don't think it was an accident?' I asked eagerly.

'Not likely! The world of theatre is fraught with rivalry, I can tell you! More drama offstage than on, and that's a fact,' said Mary. 'Ask any of the actors, they'll tell you the same.'

'So you believe someone may have wanted to harm my father?'

'Ignatius! No! I can't imagine that, my love. Never met a kinder man. Kindness goes a long way with me.' She looked about her conspiratorially, as though she half expected someone to be hiding in the room, listening. 'My theory is, it's not him they were after!'

'Really?' I realised with a twinge of surprise that we had not even considered this possibility.

'It's who might have wanted to hurt *me*, you need to be asking yourselves. Not being funny, like, but there are . . . jealousies afoot.'

'Go on,' urged Belle, her face betraying nothing.

The actress patted her hair. 'Let's just say that there's quite a few that had their eye on the role of Desdemona and auditioned for it, too. Caused quite a stir when Mr Garrick offered me the part.'

Mary Robinson was clearly enjoying herself. She opened a pot of powdered cloves, dipped in a long thin brush and began to darken her eyebrows. The effect made her look rather stern. I picked up her hairbrush absent-mindedly and ran my finger over its bristles. It would not have passed through my thick coils. I thought of our long family hair wash evenings spent with Mama, Frances, Kitty and my own Mary, oiling and braiding each other's tresses. I wondered who helped Belle look after her hair.

'Like who, Miss Robinson?' asked Belle.

The actress leaned over and gave it her best stage whisper. 'Susanna Lamont, for a start.' She snorted and turned back to the looking glass. 'Stuck-up, she is,' she said, scooping a fingerful of scarlet wax from a jar and rubbing it on to her lips. 'An old-timer. Knows Mr Garrick from way back. No sense of sisterhood. Wouldn't put it past her to try and sabotage the show and kill me stone dead into the bargain. We women should be looking out for each other, not going round dropping thumping great lamps on each other!'

She crossed the room to where a large sky-blue satin dress stood stiffly on a mannequin in a riot of ribbons, bows, and lace trimmings. She eased it off the blank-faced doll and waved to us to come and hold it still while she climbed into it.

'A theatre life's not easy for any of us,' Mary Robinson went on, one hand on my back, one hand on Belle's. 'People read the gossip columns and think we're kept women, mistresses and all that. Them newspapers! Always printing stories about how we live off men, as though we don't earn our own money! It's what the papers don't tell you that you need to worry about! Half the time it's the other way around, and we're supporting the men!'

She wriggled the dress up over her shoulders. Belle moved behind her to tie her bodice strings.

'I had a run-in with a duke once,' the actress went on. 'No names, of course. It was all roses to begin with, believe me. Tighter, love, tighter. He was very attentive, he was. I wasn't in it for the money, mind. Wealthy family, but they didn't trust him a jot with their cash. Gambling habit. Money slipped through his fingers like eels in warm water. Tighter, go on girl, don't be shy! So there's me on stage every night, trying to make ends meet, and the next thing I know, I'm paying off His Lordship's gambling debts! Hundreds of pounds' worth, it was and all!'

She took a deep breath and exhaled hard, emptying her lungs of air so that Belle could tie the final bow as tightly as possible.

'What I say is – ooh, steady on darling, what you trying to do, cut me in two? – make sure you get yourself a good job and make sure you've always got a little bit of money just for you,' said Miss Robinson, a little breathlessly. 'If you marry, stash some away. The law says whatever is ours becomes theirs when we marry them.'

She looked over her shoulder at Belle, hands on the dressing table in front of her, legs braced as though she were about to give birth. 'You should get your uncle on to that, sweetheart. That law wants changing!'

'But Susanna Lamont,' I persisted. 'You really think she might mean you harm?'

'Well, for starters, she threatened me once. Said I'd taken up with her fella. She'd been on the sauce, if you ask me. Threatened to box my ears! The cheek of it. I didn't even like the look of him. But then we both auditioned for this part and, well – there's no arguing with talent,' Miss Robinson said lightly. 'It's not as if she even needs the money. It's a vanity project, that's what it is. She's sitting on a fortune. Very shady about where the money comes from. She's got a country lodge out Surrey way. And another one up in Northumberland. Great big houses full of Louis Quinze chairs, paintings, silver, you name it. Collects servants like they're going out of fashion, they say.'

She scooped her heavy hair up in her hands and twisted it into a bun. 'Always hanging about in them coffee houses. Especially the Jamaica, over at Cornhill. I wouldn't be seen dead in there. Susanna Lamont's spoilt rotten and she's a gossip, plain and simple. Ears flapping round everyone's business and then prancing off to *Town and Country* magazine to pass on titbits to the Tête-à-Tête pages. What a way to earn a living! Here, help me on with this wig, if you please!'

What I had initially mistaken for a sleeping dog was, in fact, a large grey wig. Together, Belle and I lifted it into the air and gently lowered it over Mary's own curls. Instantly, she was three feet taller and looked another ten years older.

'Right!' she said. 'I'd best get on stage or Garrick'll have my guts for garters! He don't pay me to sit about chatting to two lovelies like you all day! How do I look?'

'Marvellous, Miss Robinson!' said Belle, stepping back to take her in. 'You'll knock their socks off.'

Mary Robinson grinned, curtsied, took a deep breath and glided, sideways, out of the door that I held open for her.

When she was gone, Belle turned to me. 'It's funny,' she said. 'The newspapers and magazines describe her as difficult. But I didn't find her difficult at all!'

'Well . . .' I said, scanning the news sheet that Mary had left behind. 'You can't believe everything you read in the press.'

Chapter Thirty-Two

The minute Mary Robinson was out of sight, we set off for Fleet Street, in the direction of the Jamaica Coffee House. It was obvious that she couldn't stand Susanna Lamont. But what did Susanna Lamont think of her? We would have to speak to her directly to find out. But Miss Robinson's interpretation of events had confused me.

'Do you think, Belle, that the chandelier was perhaps meant for Miss Robinson after all?' I asked as we walked together.

'It's possible, I suppose,' said Belle. 'But then, why would the Shadow have come to your shop if not to spy on your father?'

The Jamaica Coffee House was situated on the eastern side of the city, beyond the great dome of St Paul's. It nestled in the shadow of the Bank of England and the nearby Royal

Exchange, from which it drew the majority of its clientele. The grand piazza of the Exchange gleamed in the midday sun. Merchants had left their offices to promenade in the cool shade of the colonnades, where they barked and brayed at each other about prospects, investments and returns.

On the surface of it, people gathered at the Jamaica Coffee House for the same reasons that they did any other coffee house: to read the newspapers, to exchange information and gossip, and to close deals, all while supping cups of the dark, bitter, waking drink.

Along the back wall ran a long hearth, where the flames of a magnificent fire flickered and danced, throwing eerie shadows across the walls. On a neat row of brick towers, black cast-iron coffee pots stood in clouds of bitter, earthy smoke that smelled like Saturday mornings in the shop. Long wooden tables ran along each edge of the room, where men sat engrossed in conversation. Some brandished sheaves of paper above their heads, shouting and thumping the table with their fists. Others smoked long clay pipes as they savoured the ebony-brown drink that gave jolt to their limbs and animation to their conversation.

Two young women moved with brisk efficiency between the bar, the hearth and the tables, carrying trays loaded with steaming pots and china cups. Their faces were fixed with quiet concentration, or blank with boredom.

We stood by the door for a moment, unsure of our next move. What was it about this place that didn't quite sit right?

I scanned the room carefully. Ours were the only brown faces in sight. And on closer inspection, aside from us and the young women waiting at tables, there were barely any other women in the room. Belle's hand reached for mine and we walked slowly, side by side, across the floor to an empty table. The noisy chatter subsided to faint murmurs, and I felt the heat rise to my cheeks as every gaze in the room turned to follow us.

Every gaze but one.

A woman, seated alone in the corner, stared out of the window, silhouetted by the sun's late morning light. The emerald velvet dress she wore was matched by a deep-green hat perched on her head on an elegant slant, a bright-cerise ribbon tied around it in a magnificent bow. Her lips were painted a deep, matching shade of cherry.

As though she could feel our eyes on her, she turned her head slowly and I recognised Susanna Lamont. On seeing us, she broke into a golden smile and beckoned us over. On her lap sat curled her small glossy King Charles spaniel, into whose panting mouth she pushed sugar lumps from the table. Its quick pink tongue lolled and rolled around her slender fingers. Around its neck it wore a tiny silver locket, oval-shaped.

'Lizzie!' said Miss Lamont. 'Dear Lizzie Sancho! And if I'm not mistaken, Miss Dido Belle? Please, please sit down!'

Her voice was languid, confident. She clearly felt more at home in here than we did.

'Good afternoon, Miss Lamont. I hope you are well.' I chose my words carefully, conscious of making the right impression so that the actress would open up to us. 'We wondered if you could spare a few moments.'

She gestured for us to sit down.

'We're interviewing the great actors of the day for *Stage Door* magazine,' said Belle. 'Hoping to get the insider view on life in the theatre – in particular, on women working on the London stage. Would you be so kind as to answer some questions about your – extraordinary – work?'

Miss Lamont's mouth fell open and she put a hand to her throat as if we had just told her she had won the Leading Lady of the Year award. 'An interview!' she said. 'How exciting!'

Belle brought out her paper and quill. She cleared her throat. 'Perhaps you could describe your experiences of performing in *Othello*, with Mr Sancho?'

'Well, let's see now . . .' Miss Lamont's eyes flicked up to the corner of the room. 'I expect you already know that I play Emilia, Iago's wife. Of course, I usually take the leading role, but on this occasion, the role of Desdemona . . .'

She hesitated. Stung, no doubt, by Mary Robinson's success in landing the role?

'It must have been . . . disappointing for you to see Miss Robinson take the lead role on this occasion?' Belle prompted.

Susanna Lamont picked up the silver spoon lying on the table and plunged it into the sugar bowl. She scooped one, two, three spoonfuls of sugar into her cup of coffee. She smiled to herself as she stirred the coffee slowly, then gave the spoon three sharp raps on the side of the cup, before laying it down on the table.

'Do you know, I was actually very happy for her?' she said. 'Dear Mary. With her, shall we say, rather modern attitudes, she's far more suited to the role of Desdemona than I. You see, I rather like Emilia. She tells Othello what's what. In my opinion, Othello can get a little . . . above himself, shall we say? I believe that everyone should know their place. Emilia takes him down a peg or two.'

Something inside me tightened a notch. Miss Lamont took a sip of coffee and stared at us over the rim of the cup. I shifted in my seat. I didn't much care for being scrutinised.

'You girls. Such delightful creatures,' she oozed, laying the cup back in its saucer on the table. 'Charming. Exquisite. That hair!'

She reached a hand towards my head. I ducked away

instinctively, and my insides roiled.

Once in the shop a customer had reached across the counter and plunged her fingers into my hair at the roots without warning, that same look of mesmerised curiosity on her face. Mama was at my side in a flash, one hand holding the woman's wrist, the other held up in warning. There was fire in her eyes.

'No! Never! Ever!' she said firmly to the open-mouthed woman before disentangling her from me. The woman huffed and puffed and turned puce before turning on her heel and leaving. We never saw her again. Mama told me then in no uncertain terms never to let anyone touch my hair without express permission.

Susanna Lamont drew her hand back sharply, as though she had been slapped. She was clearly unaccustomed to being refused. Her eyes flashed with indignation for a split second, then she gave out a brittle laugh. 'Well. You are quite charming, and no mistake! Spirited, too!'

'You Elizabeth Sancho?'

A young woman appeared at our table. She wore a white apron over her green worsted dress and carried a wooden tray. On top was a sealed letter: Elizabeth Sancho and Dido Belle written on the front in a large, looping script.

'Message from the gentleman who just left . . .' the waitress said, a wry smile playing at the edges of her lips.

I slipped the letter from the tray and the girl turned away with her nose in the air. I prised the wax seal apart with my index finger and unfolded the thick paper.

In brown ink, written in large great curlicues were the words:

I SAID STOP!

An icy finger traced a path down my spine.

I jumped up and ran over to the window. I looked up and down the street. The scene was disconcertingly ordinary. People passed back and forth, but I could not see anyone I recognised. No one seemed to be in a hurry to get away, and no one seemed to be watching. I turned back to the table, folded the letter away and thrust it into my pocket, determined not to let it rattle me.

'Oh dear!' said Susanna Lamont, caressing her spaniel's ears. 'Bad news?'

It was time to leave.

'You'll have to excuse us, Miss Lamont,' I said. 'We must take our leave of you . . .'

'Not at all!' she said, pushing up on to her feet suddenly. 'In fact, I have some urgent business of my own to attend to.' Her words struck the air like hail on flagstones. 'It is *I* who must bid *you* goodbye.'

She scattered a handful of coins on the table, scooped up the spaniel and glided towards a door at the back of the room, the silk of her dress rustling in her wake. She turned briefly and flashed a feline smile at us before closing the door behind her. The sign on the door read: *Auction Room*.

Chapter Thirty-Three

33

Stepping out into the street felt like coming up from a dark river for air. As though we could finally breathe again. The cold grey light of afternoon had sunk into a bluer hue. Our conversation with Susanna Lamont had left a nasty taste in my mouth.

We walked up Fleet Street in silence for a long while, before Belle turned on me, her brow working furiously.

'What was in that letter, Lizzie, and why didn't you show me?'

I had no choice. I pulled out the letter from my right-hand pocket and handed it to her.

She shrugged. 'This doesn't make any sense.'

I pulled out the first anonymous letter I had received and gave that to her as well.

Her eyes widened almost to bursting. 'What on earth!

How long have you had this?'

'A few days . . .'

'A few days! And when – exactly, might I ask – were you going to tell me?'

'I . . . I didn't want to worry you,' I mumbled.

'Don't patronise me, Lizzie!' said Belle. I smarted at the slicing edge in her voice. 'We're in this together, aren't we? I thought we were a team. If we're being threatened, I think I ought to know about it!'

She shook her head and marched up the street ahead of me. Deep down I knew she was right. But even just a few days ago, things had felt different between us. I was still getting used to the idea of working with someone.

At the end of Fetter Lane, Belle stopped suddenly. She beckoned me over and whispered warily, 'Look! It's my carriage!'

There, in a stables behind Red Lion Court, was a carriage that looked exactly like Belle's, with the Mansfield coat of arms on the door.

'What on earth is it doing here?' Belle said.

We both saw him in the same instant. Joshua. He cast an anxious glance over his shoulder and disappeared into a narrow doorway. Above it, an iron sign swung and creaked in the wind. *Guinea Coffee House.*

We pulled the hoods of our cloaks up over our heads and scanned the room for Joshua as we made our way across the floor of the Guinea Coffee House. The crowd inside was markedly different from the one we had just left behind. The people here seemed to hail from all corners of the globe: faces of all hues, and languages galore. One table conversed in French, another in Arabic. In the corner a table of Jewish scholars, discussing politics. Another group bantered in the light patois Mama used when among certain friends. This was more like the London I knew. Taking care to keep our faces hidden from view, we passed a table of women deep in conversation, their voices punchy with urgency.

'They say he works fast. There's another gone this week.'

'What about the Law? Where are they when you need them?'

'The Bow Street Runners haven't lifted a finger on this yet. Have you heard, though? Sancho is back at Drury Lane – *Othello* opens next week.'

'About time too! Why have we waited so long, that's what I want to know. It's one excuse after another.'

'You know why – they're still dragging their heels over abolishing the slave trade in Parliament. You think they want people to see one of our men – a Black man – delivering powerful speeches up on that great big stage?'

Belle grabbed my arm and tilted her head to the left. There was Joshua, slipping behind a grey curtain. What on earth was he up to?

We sat down at a table just outside the curtain. From here, we could hear what sounded like a meeting in progress.

'Next, I'd like to welcome Brother Ottobah Cugoano to the group.' A man's voice, sombre. His accent bore the West African tinge I had heard among my parents' friends. 'Brother Ottobah is a Fanti man from Ajumako. He laboured in Grenada and has been here in London for a few years now. He is a gifted writer and is working on an anti-slavery tract. Please welcome our brother.'

There was a round of applause. Seven, eight people perhaps? Judging by the calls of approval and welcome, a mix of women and men.

'So. On to our updates. First, we must address with renewed urgency the issue of the Vanishings. Our brothers and sisters are being snatched from their homes, from the streets, by these bounty hunters. Some are sent to work in bondage in country homes across the land. Dressed up and collared, like pets.'

There were murmurs of disgust.

'Some are sent to plantations in the Caribbean to labour in enslavement, with little hope of return. I'm sorry to report that we have recently lost another young brother to the bounty hunters. There's one bounty hunter in particular we are after. Wilkins. We have an undercover operative on his tail, but Wilkins is proving slippery.'

'But Brother Ezekiel, what about the Bow Street Runners?' piped up a younger man's voice. 'Why aren't they helping us?'

'That's two more this week,' said an elderly woman's voice in exasperation. 'This is getting out of hand!'

'Kofi was taken from his own bed, they said,' the younger man replied. There's one of them that always comes in the night.'

Kofi – that was *Mercury*! No! So that was what had happened to him! My head swam. How could I have not realised that he was gone? Every day I had simply expected to see him. I gripped Belle's hand and squeezed it.

'We can't keep losing people this way,' the man they called Brother Ezekiel insisted. 'The *Apollo* sails out to Barbados a week on Sunday. If we don't find them before then, well . . . they'll be gone to us forever.'

There was a silence while those words sank in.

'And so,' Ezekiel continued with a sigh, 'we *must* keep searching the dockyards until we find where he's keeping them.'

'*And* we need weapons if we're going to send in a rescue party.' That was Joshua's voice! Belle looked over at me, open-mouthed.

'Have we got the manpower for that?' the older woman asked.

'Well, let's find out.' Joshua again. 'I suggest that anyone who can help us with an ambush on the docks meets us tomorrow night to plan the attack.'

Brother Ezekiel cut in once more. 'All right, everyone, listen up now. What's next on the agenda? Ah yes, the posters warning people about the bounty hunters. Our good sister here has offered to distribute posters throughout St Giles's parish, all the way over to Bloomsbury. Over to you, Sister . . .'

'Thank you, Brother Ezekiel.' A young woman's voice. It sounded so very much like – 'So as our good brother here was saying, we've already sent word to comrades in the streets to the north of here . . .'

The speaker paused to arrange her papers. That voice! It couldn't be!

'Our next drop will be around Soho. We need to spread the word, fast!'

It was, without a shadow of doubt.

Frances!

Chapter Thirty-Four

I held my breath. Should I make myself known to Frances or not? I didn't want to risk stopping the meeting.

Ezekiel spoke again.

'We are, first and foremost, a community organisation. This is a collective effort. My thanks also to Brother Joshua for offering to deliver our messages across the city.'

Belle shook her head in disbelief.

The chairman went on. 'We all know that Brother Joshua is deepening his knowledge of the law, thanks to his proximity to the Chief Justice Lord Mansfield. So far, our endeavours have been almost exclusively underground. But we have to fight this battle on as many fronts as possible. We may have to consider leaning a little harder on Mansfield. He passed the Somerset ruling. That's the law the bounty hunters are violating.'

The young man's voice piped up again: 'We can't rely on the Establishment to help us! They know very well what's going on. They just don't care. We need to stick to our own methods, our own means.'

'Why shouldn't they help us though?' The older woman. 'They've got the money, the resources. Let's not forget where that money comes from! Our labour on the plantations. We should claim what's rightfully ours. We need horses, weapons, if we're to really fight this thing.'

I had so many questions. Did Belle's Uncle William know about the Vanishings? What did they mean, '*Lean a little harder on Mansfield*'? And what about my parents? Did they know Frances was here? They clearly knew about Mercury. Why hadn't anyone told Belle and me about this?

The sound of chairs scraping on the wood told us that they were preparing to leave. We pulled our hoods over our eyes and bent low over the table towards one another. One by one, the speakers emerged from behind the curtain. They passed through the room, laying down posters and pamphlets on every table. People turned and nodded, shook hands. Some stood as the group passed, placing their fists over their chests as I had seen Joshua and Papa do.

Outside the window, they embraced each other and

went their separate ways. We watched as Frances pulled her hood up over her head and disappeared around the corner, out of sight.

Belle shook her head. 'I can't believe it,' she said. 'Joshua. He's a freedom fighter, Lizzie! And your sister! Did you know?'

I shook my head. I'd had no idea whatsoever. And now I was wondering what else I did not know.

I picked up a handful of pamphlets from a nearby table.

A MESSAGE FROM THE SONS AND DAUGHTERS OF AFRICA

Campaigners for the Abolition of the Slave Trade and Freedom Fighters

RESISTANCE – FREEDOM – COMMUNITY

MISSING

KOFI, also known as MERCURY

13 years old, of middling height, with short black hair and a scar above his right eyebrow.

Last seen on Saturday 12th April when he completed his round of newspaper deliveries.

Believed to have gone missing from Red Lion Court between Saturday evening and Monday morning.

Any news or information, please post immediately to Sancho's Tea Shop and Grocer's, Charles Street, Westminster.

His employer, Bill Weekes, editor of the *Daily Advertiser*, has shut up shop and is rumoured to have travelled out of London.

WANTED!

Beware this man. He is a bounty hunter, a trader in enslavement working on the streets of London. He kidnaps the vulnerable and sells them off to the highest bidders to be held enslaved in country houses or in the plantations of the West Indies.

He is a danger to our communities and must be caught.

Do <u>not</u> approach him if you are alone.

His name: WILKINS

And there, below the warning, was a picture of the face that had been haunting me for the last week.

Hooded eyes, a heavy jaw. The mouth, twisted into a cruel sneer as if disgusted with life and everything it had to offer.

It was a face made ugly from within.

It was the Shadow.

ACT IV

Chapter Thirty-Five

35

I could hardly believe it. The man who had tried to kill my father was called Wilkins, and he was a bounty hunter! Kidnapping people – young people – from the streets, from their homes, and selling them into enslavement. A trader. I stared into the cold eyes in the illustration. Knowing that he was still out there filled me with terror. He had taken Mercury . . . Poor Mercury. Where was he? I hoped that wherever he was, he wasn't alone or afraid.

We had to get back to the theatre, and fast. But what would I tell Papa? Did he know about Frances' involvement with the Sons and Daughters of Africa? Should I speak with her? But so far, no one had involved me in their conversations about the Vanishings. Would they believe me? If they suspected for a moment that I was also trying to track down a dangerous criminal like Wilkins, they would not let me out of their sight.

As we left the Guinea Coffee House, thunderous black clouds rumbled and swelled in the sky. Unable to contain their rage any longer, they burst in a tumultuous sound clash, loosing their anger on to the streets below. Water pelted mercilessly on to the crowds that hurried through the streets, their wooden clogs clattering and sliding on the cobbles as they sought shelter in doorways from the relentless rain. Belle and I clung to each other as we raced along, for comfort as much as for support.

We turned into Drury Lane. Across the road stood a thin figure huddled in a doorway, their eyes fixed on us. Was it a cutpurse, hoping to steal our money? Or someone working for one of the bounty hunters the freedom fighters had been speaking of?

The figure darted across the street towards us and I saw that it was just a boy, small, skinny.

'Puck!' I gasped. 'You frightened me! What are you doing skulking about after us like that?'

Puck's head switched like a small bird's in every direction as he spoke. 'Not here! We need to find somewhere safe to talk . . .'

We ran west towards Seven Dials, hooded and huddled together against the rain. We ducked into the church of St Giles in the Fields, which stood at the centre of the Parish and was a safe haven for anyone who chose to enter, no matter what their beliefs. Swaggering clouds swelled darkly overhead.

'This way!' Puck called above the din of the driving rain.

We passed through an iron gate into the churchyard. The black yew trees blocked out the moonlight and the moss-covered gravestones leaned dangerously close to the ground. We pushed through the tall, arched doors into the church and they swung closed behind us with a resounding bang. The sound echoed through the vaulted hall, breaking the serenity of the cool stone chamber.

We shook the rain out of our clothes and slipped into a pew at the back. The air was thick with the woody fragrance of burning incense. At the front of the church knelt a solitary cloaked woman, her head resting on clasped hands.

'Lizzie, there's still no sign of Tom!' Puck whispered. 'He hasn't gone back to his room and no one has seen him for days.'

Belle and I exchanged nervous glances. I took one of the pamphlets out from under my cloak and showed Wilkins' picture to Puck.

'Puck, this is the man who dropped the chandelier from the balcony.'

Puck looked at me in disbelief. 'How do you know?'

'Belle and I saw him that night,' I said. 'We didn't see

his face. But since then, he's been hanging around outside the shop, outside the theatre. It's definitely him. His name is Wilkins.'

'We have to tell someone!' said Puck.

I looked at Belle.

'We're not the only people looking for him,' Belle said. 'The Sons and Daughters of Africa are on his tail. They're abolitionists, freedom fighters. We've just come from one of their secret meetings.'

Puck thought for a moment. 'If we know that this is the man who tried to murder your father, then surely it's safe for Tom to come home?' he said. 'It means he's definitely innocent!'

I took a deep breath. This was not going to be easy.

'Puck . . .' I laid my hand on his arm. 'This man is a bounty hunter. He's been kidnapping people and selling them to slave traders. Look!' I showed him the page about Mercury. 'We . . . we think that Wilkins is also the man who took Tom.'

Puck's eyes widened with fright. 'Took him? What do you mean? I thought he had run away!'

'We found this in the Tower.' I pulled out the piece of paper with Tom's address on it. 'Someone must have told Wilkins where he could find Tom . . .'

Puck jumped to his feet. 'We have to find Tom! We can't let this happen to him!'

The woman at the front turned on us with a disapproving look and hissed a 'Shhhh!'

'And we will find him.' I kept my voice low. 'Here, take some of these pamphlets and talk to everyone you know. The more ground we can cover, the sooner we can find them.'

'And,' Belle added, 'Brother Ezekiel said that they had an undercover operative tracking Wilkins. But the Sons and Daughters of Africa are after Wilkins because he's a bounty hunter. They don't know that he's the Shadow. They don't know that they need to protect Mr Sancho from him as well as the poor wretches he is stealing from the streets.'

No, they don't, I thought to myself miserably. Only we knew that. High above our heads, the arched windows held stories of saints frozen in coloured glass: red, yellow, blue, green, their faces turned upwards towards the skies.

'Come on,' I said, standing up. 'We need to get back to the theatre. They'll be wondering where we are.'

When we left the church, the rain had stopped. It had done its job of emptying the streets of people. Now they were desolate, bereft of all human life. The three of us trudged back to the theatre in silence, heads bowed.

Maybe it was the way the fog seemed to swim around us in the indigo darkness of the night. Or the way my dread pushed down on me like a weight of water from above.

But as we made our way back through the silent streets to the theatre, I felt as though I were sinking into a deep, dark ocean. I longed to kick up towards the surface for air, but with no light in sight, I had no idea which direction to turn.

Charles Street
Westminster
London

Saturday 19th April 1777

Dear Belle,

Mama says that I must stay home and help in the
shop for the next few days. I understand now that
they are concerned about the bounty hunters, but
she and Papa seem to think that our late arrival
at the theatre last night justifies shutting me out
from any adult conversation. They whisper in
corners constantly. And yet I am the only person in
the house that knows that Wilkins is the man who
tried to kill Papa!

It's strange – my father believes he is protecting me by keeping me here at home, but I feel that I must get back out on to the streets so that I can protect _him_!

People I now recognise as members of the Sons and Daughters of Africa come and go, leaving messages, exchanging news in hushed voices. Our community is shot through with fear. I cannot sleep for worrying about Mercury. Where is Wilkins keeping him? And Tom too? How on earth are we going to find them?

One question that troubles me is this: if Wilkins is a bounty hunter, trading in enslaved people – why would he try and _kill_ my father, rather than take him, like the others?

When can we next meet, I wonder?

Your friend,
Lizzie

Saturday 19th April, 1777

Kenwood House
Hampstead Heath
London

My dearest Lizzie,

Do not despair – it seems we are to have some time together here at Kenwood!

Did you know that your father is coming to visit Uncle William on Tuesday? Apparently, they have some important business together, though Uncle William will not share with me what it is. He says I am 'not to worry my pretty little head' about it. However, he has agreed to my inviting you to come with your father.

Do you suppose they will discuss the Vanishings?

We must find a way to listen in on their conversation! Any extra information we can glean from them could be crucial to solving the case.

In response to your questions, I am also thinking – is it possible perhaps that Wilkins intentionally framed Tom, that he wanted everyone to believe that it was Tom who had dropped the chandelier? Like you, I am confused about his motive for dropping the chandelier in the first place. I keep thinking back to what Mr Ash said about motive. What moves someone to act? What moved Wilkins to do what he did?

I enclose an updated version of the case notes. If we can work out Wilkins' motive, surely we can present these notes as evidence and have him arrested.

Do not despair. We are getting closer, I know it . . .

Aunt Betty says that Joshua will come for you both with the coach at midday.

Until then, always, your dear friend,
Belle

Updated NOTES on The Othello Case

- **Crime:** Attempted murder?
- **Intended victim:** Ignatius Sancho
- **Scene:** Stage balcony, Theatre Royal
- **Weapon:** Chandelier, dropped from a great height
- **Time and date:** Friday 11th April, 1777, around 8 of the clock, evening

Prime suspect:
WILKINS – previously known as The Shadow.
Tall man, broad-shouldered, wears black caped coat, black tri-cornered hat, smells of tobacco.
KNOWN BOUNTY HUNTER, DANGEROUS

Did he take Mercury? Has he taken Tom?
Where does he keep people hidden?

Sightings:
Friday 11th April
- A minute or so before 5 o'clock in road by stage door
- At around 8 o'clock, on balcony above stage

Saturday 12th April
- At around 8 o'clock, outside Sancho's shop

Wednesday 16th April

- At around half past 1 o'clock at theatre, suspect entered by the stage door (has key?)
- After an hour or so in theatre (where? with whom??) suspect left by stage door and proceeded east towards Fleet Street
- Suspect turned and faced Lizzie, then disappeared into crowd

Secondary suspect:
Meg – Who is she?

Sightings:

Monday 14th April

- Snooping around balcony in morning
- Warned Lizzie away from crime scene, asked if she'd found anything

Wednesday 16th April

On Fleet Street

- Travelling to meeting with the Shadow?
- Following Lizzie?
- May be known to Sancho family?
- Motive: unknown

Also questioned:

Garrick

- Theatre manager, actor, friend to Mr Sancho
- Very nervous, not keen to share information
- Keen to go ahead with production (even if not safe?)
- Protecting Tom
- On stage at the time of the crime

Greenwoode

- Assistant director, always at odds with Garrick
- Melancholic and intense by turns
- Seems concerned for Mr Sancho
- Believes it may have been attempted murder
- Suspects Tom
- On stage at the time of the crime

Ash

- Saved Mr Sancho's life (unlikely suspect)
- Spoke of rift between Garrick and Greenwoode, rivalry between Mary Robinson and Susanna Lamont

Mary Robinson

- believes the chandelier may have been meant for her
- vehement dislike for Susanna Lamont
- suspicious when knew she was going to be questioned, but answered questions without further hesitation

Susanna Lamont

- Expressed dislike for the character of Othello
- Said some strange things about Mary Robinson
- Tried to touch Lizzie's hair

MISSING

~~Tom Johnson, stagehand~~

- ~~Tall, like the Shadow seen on the balcony Friday 11th, and the figure spotted outside Sancho's shop on Saturday 12th.~~
- ~~Was responsible for chandelier on the night~~
- ~~Disappeared immediately after the event (according to Greenwoode)~~
- ~~Motive: unknown~~

Tom was last 'heard' at home by Puck, through his door, on the evening of Friday 11 April, after chandelier had fallen.

Possible that Tom was **never at the theatre** that night.

Someone (Shadow from balcony? Meg?) had his address, dropped it in Tower.

- Who wrote it down? Was someone sent to Tom's house?
- Tom's keys to the theatre were still in his room.
- Where is Tom now??

MISSING

Kofi / Mercury, messenger and newspaper delivery boy
- SDOA believe Wilkins or another bounty hunter responsible

Chapter Thirty-Seven

O n Tuesday morning, the day I was to visit Belle, it was raining again. Gazing out of my window on to the sodden streets below, I felt glad of the chance to spend the day at Kenwood and share my thoughts with my friend in person.

And what of Papa and Lord Mansfield? Had they met before, I wondered? Were they planning to discuss the production, or would they speak only of the Vanishings? Would Papa tell Lord Mansfield about the Sons and Daughters of Africa? Perhaps he was going to do the 'leaning' that they had spoken of at the Guinea Coffee House.

Looking down from my window, I saw that Joshua had arrived with the coach. He stood outside the shop door, deep in conversation with a young woman in the street, a shawl drawn tightly over her head and shoulders to protect her from the driving rain. It beat down in heavy sheets, obscuring my view. Through the rivulets pouring down the pane I could just make out the woman laying her hand on Joshua's shoulder. He drew her towards him: his words, silent to me, seemed earnest, entreating. She pushed away from him suddenly, handed him a bag, and disappeared into the shop.

I dashed down the stairs to intercept her. She stood by the door with her back to me, shaking out her shawl, damp from the rain. Sensing she was being observed, she turned suddenly to face me. Frances! When would she stop surprising me like this!

'Frances!' I gasped. 'Where have you been? And what were you doing out there with –'

'Sssshhh!' Frances grabbed me by the elbow and pulled me to the side of the room. Mama was out at the market and Papa was upstairs getting ready for our visit to Kenwood. It was Frances' day on duty in the shop. 'Not so loud, Lizzie!'

'But – what were you talking about? What did you give to Joshua?'

Would she tell me the truth, I wondered? She did not yet know that *I* knew she was a Daughter of Africa.

'Nothing! Never you mind!'

'It didn't look like nothing from where I was standing!'

Frances sighed. She tried another angle. 'That is to

say – it's *work*. And it's nothing for you to worry about.'

Why did people keep on telling me and Belle that this was nothing for us to worry about?

'What work?' I asked, an edge of challenge in my voice.

'Please, Lizzie, just trust me.'

I did trust her. But I wanted to know what she was up to.

'Is this to do with why you were at the Guinea Coffee House?'

Frances' mouth fell open. She looked around furtively and pulled me further into the corner. 'What makes you think I was at the Guinea Coffee House?' Her voice was all warning.

I calculated swiftly. 'Are you saying you *weren't* there?'

She folded her arms and gave me such a look that for a moment it was as though Mama herself were standing over me.

Two could play at that game.

'We saw you, Belle and I,' I said. 'At the Sons and Daughters of Africa meeting. We overheard the whole thing!'

Frances hauled in a huge gasp of air. 'What! You are not – I repeat *not* – to speak to anyone of that, do you hear me, Lizzie? For your own safety! And anyway, what on earth were *you* doing in there?'

'Theatre business!' I said defiantly.

Frances gave me another sceptical look. She had a vast array of them. 'What theatre business?'

'I can't tell you any more than that for now, *for your own safety*,' I replied, enjoying myself now. 'But you'll find out soon enough.'

Frances took me by the shoulders and held me squarely in her view. 'Careful, Lizzie. I mean it. London's a dangerous place for people like us right now. You need to stay off the streets and keep out of trouble. Do you understand?'

I held my head high. 'Stop worrying about me. Anyway Joshua's going to drive us around from now on.'

'Yes, so I hear,' said Frances tartly. 'As if he hasn't got enough on his plate!'

I decided to ignore that.

'So *tell* me what I need to be afraid of,' I challenged. 'I think I'm safer if I know more about the dangers I'm facing, no? And I want to know what you know.' Now I hesitated. 'I felt . . . I felt . . . proud when I saw you in there.'

She sighed and dropped down into the nearest chair, gesturing for me to sit opposite her. Then she gathered herself, fixed her thoughts and explained.

'We're an underground organisation. Our main objective is the freedom of our people, plain and simple. We work towards the total – emancipation – of people – of African – descent.' She marked each beat on the table with the side of her right hand.

'Slavery is a wicked horror, Lizzie. Our people have organised rebellions on plantations; they've put their lives at risk by running away. Even learning to read and write holds great risk for the enslaved. We are under attack on all sides – we have to be flexible in the ways in which we fight back.'

What Frances was saying echoed in so many ways things I had heard my mother say, my father say. Maybe it was not so surprising that she was a freedom fighter after all.

She grasped my hands and held my gaze with hers as she spoke. 'Mansfield's Somerset ruling gave everyone some hope that if we were *here*, our safety was guaranteed. But that's changing. We're pushing hard towards the abolition of slavery, but slave traders are pulling in the other direction. And the bounty hunters are taking their work underground. We need to increase our resistance – on *every* front.'

I flinched and thought of Mercury, then of Tom. No one had mentioned Tom during the meeting.

Suddenly, my cheeks were burning and tears pricked my eyes. I realised then that I had to tell Frances about Tom's disappearance. Perhaps the Sons and Daughters of Africa were his only chance of survival.

So I told her. I told her all about the night at the theatre, and about Puck and about going to Tom's house and his not being there.

Strangely, I did not tell her about Wilkins. About how I had chased him. About how he had the eyes of a shark. As though he would have bitten me in two had he caught me. Perhaps I knew that if I told her, she would not have let me leave the house again.

Frances listened attentively, deep in thought. Her brows met in that way they did whenever she was concentrating hard, or feeling anxious, or both. She nodded to herself, as though making a decision.

Then she stepped back from me to do 'the check', wiping the last tears from my face with her handkerchief, and smoothing back the bushed mass of my hair from my forehead.

'Go on, you'd better get along. Joshua's waiting.' Her voice was like velvet. 'I'll hurry Papa along.'

I climbed into the coach, aching to ask Joshua about his involvement with my sister, but he was staring resolutely ahead in a way that did not invite conversation. Papa climbed in beside me, Joshua snapped the reins and we were off.

The carriage rolled and rumbled through the uneven streets. Papa took my hand and held it tightly throughout the journey, but he did not say a word. Did he know about Frances and Joshua? He certainly seemed to like Joshua. However, Frances had seemed pretty serious about me not saying anything. I would just have to wait and wonder for now.

As the carriage pulled up the hill towards Hampstead Heath, the clouds began to clear and a few rays of sun pushed their way through the gaps in the grey, shining in great straight beams that cast a pale yellow light on the house and the fields that stretched out green and wonderful around it. Here and there, people strolled arm in arm in twos and threes – not a care among them, it seemed. The trees shimmered, their shining wet leaves vibrant against the sky. The air smelled fresh and clean, hopeful with the gentle fragrance of summer grass.

What was it about the Heath that momentarily pushed troubled thoughts aside and overwhelmed you instead with the undeniable beauty of its ancient trees, its wide hills, its emerald ponds, its waving grasses?

As though, whatever was happening out there on the streets of London, here in this place, one could always find space, life, breath, peace.

Chapter Thirty-Eight

'Oh my life! Such beauty!' exclaimed Papa, as the coach pulled up the drive towards Kenwood House. He adjusted his cuffs and smoothed down the front of his waistcoat. I smiled inwardly, remembering how nervous I had been for my first meeting with Belle.

Joshua jumped down to help me out of the carriage. I refused him politely and asked if he could help Papa, who was struggling to get down. Some inflammation in his left ankle was causing him considerable discomfort, but he wore it proudly, often refusing to fuss or accept any obvious attempts of help. But he took the arm that Joshua offered, and his eyes shone with gratitude. He patted Joshua's hand and I suddenly thought about how it must be for him to have so many daughters and just his one baby son. He looked older as he leaned on Joshua for support.

Would he live to see Billy grow into a man?

Belle was walking briskly towards the coach to greet us, arms outstretched. 'Such a pleasure to see you again, Mr Sancho. You are most welcome! Uncle William is looking forward to meeting you. He will receive you in the library. Tea is prepared. Thank you, Joshua.'

As we walked through the corridor, past those haughty stares on the walls, Belle flashed me a look that signalled that she had urgent news to share. And I was desperate to know what Papa wanted to discuss.

Belle opened the doors into the library. Papa gazed around him and gasped. He mopped his brow with his handkerchief and his eyes shone.

'Ah, Ignatius!' cried Lord Mansfield, getting up from his writing desk and striding towards Papa with his hand outstretched. The men greeted each other with a firm handshake. 'How good of you to come all this way!' Lord Mansfield went on, clapping Papa on the back as he spoke. 'I hope you are well. I understand you have an issue of pressing concern to discuss.'

'Indeed I do, Sir! But . . .' Papa cast a glance towards the table in the corner where we were hovering over the tea settings, trying to look busy and inconspicuous at the same time. 'It is a matter of great delicacy . . . the girls.'

Et tu, Papa?

Lord Mansfield turned to us. 'Now Belle,' he said. 'Mr Sancho and I have some grave matters to discuss. Perhaps you could show your friend –'

'Lizzie,' I said, with a curt nod.

'Of course, yes, Lizzie. Perhaps you could show Lizzie the rose garden.'

He ushered us out of the room and closed the door firmly. So much for listening in on their conversation.

I looked appealingly at Belle.

'Don't worry!' she said, taking my arm and leading me out of the house and up the hill towards the dairy. 'I have a plan!'

In the outhouse that Belle had converted into our investigation room, the tables were covered in piles of paper. Belle seemed to have gathered even more books, magazines and notes than before. She pulled a large blue volume from beneath a pile of pamphlets.

'Look!' she said breathlessly.

It was the book of architectural plans by the Adam Brothers – the one she had used to guide me to the Tower. Belle turned to an illustrated map of rooms that seemed to be connected by a series of subterranean tunnels.

'This is a plan of Kenwood House. Look, here we are in the dairy. And Uncle and your father are here, in the library.'

I squinted closely.

'You see these dotted lines?' Belle went on. 'That's the service tunnel.'

'What on earth's a service tunnel?'

'It's a tunnel that connects the kitchen to other rooms in the house so that the servants can serve dinner without having to bring it outside,' Belle explained. 'You see, the kitchen is all the way over there. When they are serving any of the family meals, Nancy and her staff take the food through this tunnel to the dining room. But look – the tunnel also leads to a secret chamber below the library.'

I stared at the map. 'Are you suggesting by any chance that we hide in that chamber and eavesdrop on the men's conversation?'

'Absolutely!'

'Genius, Belle! So where does it begin?'

She bent down and pulled back the large Turkish rug in the centre of the floor to reveal a square hatch. 'Right here under our feet,' she said in triumph. 'The first part of the tunnel runs from the dairy to the kitchen!'

Chapter Thirty-Nine

Belle brought a lit taper from the back room, shielding the flame with a cupped hand to keep it alive. I opened the hatch and eased myself from a sitting position on the edge into the small space below. In front of me was a small flight of stone steps leading downwards into darkness. I began the descent and Belle followed, closing the hatch behind us, shutting out the light.

Now it was virtually pitch black in the tunnel, but for the sickly yellow light from our small candle. I reached back for Belle's hand, grasping her cool fingers tightly, and we made our way forward, treading carefully as we went.

After a few moments, the tunnel curved around a corner. Without sight it was almost impossible to orientate ourselves properly. Belle passed in front of me with the taper and we continued on our way, following the tunnel as it wound its way onwards in the gloom.

'I can see a door!' Belle murmured.

We heard the creak of footsteps on floorboards overhead. Belle turned the handle and the door opened into a stone chamber.

'Do you think this is it?' I hissed.

Belle put her fingers to her lips. Very faintly, we could hear the sound of her uncle's voice, somewhere further off. She held the taper up in front of us. Its light flickered and struggled in the gloom.

'This way!' she whispered.

As we walked on, Lord Mansfield's voice became louder, more distinct.

'And how many exactly?' he was saying.

Then Papa's voice, low, muffled, distressed. 'I have been informed of two more this week alone. My Black sistren and brethren vanishing – literally vanishing – from their homes, from the streets. We are committing many of our own resources towards finding the bounty hunters, but it is not enough. The Bow Street Runners tell us they are overstretched. Without significant help or resources from elsewhere, we will continue to lose people. We are in a desperate situation, Sir – a desperate situation!'

A silence, followed by footsteps that reminded me of Belle's own habit of pacing when she needed to think.

Then Lord Mansfield spoke up.

'I am glad you have brought this to my attention. I had heard some word of this, but had no idea of the scale of the problem. They are operating completely outside the law, and yet in plain sight. They seem to have a very close network. And friends in high places. Whoever is at work here leaves very little trace. We've asked around at the taverns, the coffee houses . . . no one can tell us anything that can help us. Or at least, those that have spoken have disappeared soon after. We need evidence. And we need to know where they are hiding people before they smuggle them out to these houses or ship them off to plantations.'

So Lord Mansfield *did* know about the Vanishings. Who else knew? And why weren't the newspapers screaming about it?

'This simply won't do!' cried Papa. 'I implore you, Sir,' he urged, lowering his voice, 'to put more manpower on the case. You are one of the most powerful men in the land. Our people are speaking of taking up arms to defend themselves, and who can blame them? These are our children! You have access to horses, weapons . . . even soldiers. You could use your influence to raise an army!'

The men's voices moved around the room as they spoke. We followed as best we could, moving around in the half-light, trusting to our ears for direction as much as our eyes.

'We must . . .'

Lord Mansfield was talking but we could no longer make out what he was saying. I realised then that I had not heard Papa mention the Sons and Daughters of Africa by name, nor the planned ambush at the docks. Were they a secret organisation then? Did Lord Mansfield even know of their existence?

We crept around this way for almost an hour, straining our ears to pick up what conversation we could.

Eventually, the men went quiet.

Then Papa piped up, 'And where are the girls?'

We froze.

Their footsteps echoed above our heads as they crossed the floor.

We turned to follow the tunnel back to the dairy. If they were planning to go there to find us, we needed to arrive ahead of them.

'This way!' Belle said, pulling me in haste towards an open doorway that led directly into the brick-walled tunnel. She hurried along, the candle sputtering in her hand, melting away. In the dying light I could just make out the walls on either side of us, but we could see virtually nothing ahead. It were as though we were being swallowed by darkness.

Belle reached back and grasped my hand for comfort

in the deep night of that passageway. The tunnel seemed painfully narrow, much more so than I remembered on the way here. The walls pressed in against us. The ceiling was low and arched over our heads, so close that I could feel my hair catching on its rough surface.

And then – the ground underfoot, soft, as though we were walking on soil. It was as though we were walking down into the earth!

This wasn't right. How would Nancy and her team bring food along this passageway to the dining room?

Belle spoke my next thought: 'We must have taken a wrong turn!'

The candle flickered violently, as though about to take its last gasp.

We turned back, quickly retracing our steps. Would we find our way back to the chamber beneath the library? And from there to the dairy? Or the kitchen? My breathing became laboured. All I wanted now was to be above ground. We crept along swiftly, two moving as one, willing the candle to stay alive.

A sharp clang rang out just ahead of us.

The sound of steel on stone.

We stopped dead.

I dared not breathe.

Only the silence was alive.

As though it were listening to us.

And then footsteps. Slow, heavy, deliberate. Coming towards us.

My fear switched up to terror. My heart knocked against my ribcage like a trapped bird. Running was our only chance.

I grabbed Belle's arm, pulling her hard. The candle died in the rush of the moment and I thrust my hand out in front of me, feeling only air, seeing only darkness ahead as we raced and stumbled through the tunnel.

Behind us, the swift and heavy footfall gathering speed, gaining on us.

Up ahead, a square of light where Belle had left the hatch open! I let go of Belle's hand and powered towards it. I hauled myself up quickly and reached out to pull Belle up behind me. She leaped and grabbed my hand. I yanked her up into the room, rolled her across the floorboards, flipped the hatch over and slammed it shut.

A second's silence. The hatch bucked against my hand with a thud and a large hair-covered hand reached through the gap towards me. I slammed it shut, down on the fingers and they were snatched back into the darkness below with a strangled yelp of pain.

'The lock!' Belle gasped.

I shoved the wooden bolt across the slot. The hatch banged again from underneath, once, twice. We pressed down on it with all our strength.

We did not breathe.

We waited.

Silence.

Then slow, heavy footsteps retreating.

We sat there for what seemed like an age, willing our breath to return to its normal rhythm, watching the square panel of wood in the centre of the floor with concentrated intensity, as though were we to relax our guard or avert our eyes for a split second, the hatch might be flung open.

But it was over. For now.

I had the powerful sensation of having narrowly escaped the jaws of a giant ocean creature, who, disturbed from sleep, had surged hungry towards the light beyond the sea. Breaking for an instant the surface of the ocean, arching and reaching towards its prey, it had missed it mark by a hair's breadth, rolled and plunged down again into darkness, to the depths of its watery underworld.

A sharp knocking at the door sent my heart pounding. Loud, insistent. We scrambled to our feet.

'Belle? Belle, are you in there?'

'Yes, Uncle!' Belle called in a bright voice, glancing

nervously towards the open books out on the tables.

Lord Mansfield tried the door. It was locked.

'Belle! Belle, open this door at once!'

'Coming, Uncle!'

Belle flung open the door with a wide smile. 'Lizzie and I have been studying together,' she explained, waving her hand dismissively.

Lord Mansfield peered over Belle's shoulder at the books on the tables. 'Are those books from my library, Belle?'

My eyes flicked to the piles of books and magazines. Was it my imagination or did they look even more chaotic than before?

'Yes, Uncle. I – I borrowed them for my time with Lizzie. I'll return them very soon, I promise.'

Lord Mansfield frowned. 'See you take care of them. The dairy's no place for them. Mr Sancho and his daughter will be returning home shortly. Joshua will have the carriage ready in ten minutes.'

And he turned away.

Belle closed the door and rolled her eyes at me. 'If only they knew!'

But I was too stricken to answer.

'Lizzie?'

I lifted book after book, went from table to table, searching, searching, utterly in vain.

'Lizzie, what is it?' said Belle.

How could I tell her?

'Belle . . .' My voice, when it finally came, was hoarse with horror.

'Our case notes. They're gone!'

Chapter Forty

I awoke the following morning with a heavy heart. This last blow to our investigation cast the darkest shadow yet.

Now the terror of being hunted was real. Someone – Wilkins? – had chased us through those tunnels. That same person had known that we were investigating the case; they had broken into the room at the dairy; they had rifled through our belongings and had stolen our case notes.

Worse still, whoever had stolen them now knew everything we had discovered so far. This would make it easy for them to cover their tracks and send us scuttling in the wrong direction.

We were so close, but how would we solve the case now?

Downstairs, Mama was sitting calmly at the kitchen table, sorting pamphlets into two piles. I watched her from the doorway for a brief moment, marvelling at the speed and intensity with which she worked. So, delivering messages for the Sons and Daughters of Africa was practically a family business!

Meanwhile, Papa was opening and closing drawers, clearly agitated.

'Where are my glasses? Has someone moved my script?'

Bang went the door of the kitchen cupboard.

'Why is nothing ever where I left it in this house?'

It was the day of the dress rehearsal.

He sat down at the table, looking deflated and defeated.

'I don't know if I can do this, Ann dearest,' he said, rubbing his eyes. 'Is it right to even take to the stage while we are searching for our comrades?'

Mama took a long, slow breath and passed her arm around his shoulders. They leaned their heads together for a brief moment.

'Ignatius, you've got to get up on that stage on Friday,' Mama said.

Papa sighed.

'Think of all the people in that room who will see you, who will hear your voice?' she cried. 'That's not something to throw away! And you know that how they see us makes all the difference. Especially now!'

She stood and packed the pamphlets away into two bags lying on the table.

'The Sons and Daughters have all their man and womanpower on this now, Ignatius. You focus on what you can do. What you must do. Garrick's right behind you on this one, you know.'

She started when she saw me loitering in the doorway.

'Lizzie! You made me jump, darling!' She straightened her dress and patted her hair. Her voice, when she spoke again, was bright as summer sun. 'Go with your father to the theatre today and cheer him up a little, will you? I'll see you both when you get home.'

With that, she kissed us goodbye and ushered us out of the door.

Chapter Forty-One

Inside the Theatre Royal, the corridors buzzed with activity.

'Can we have musicians on stage in five for a run-through of the intro to Act Four, please! Musicians!'

'Mind your backs, ladies and gents!'

Two men pushed a huge, flat wooden garden on wheels down the corridor. I pressed myself against the wall as landscaped hedges and rosebushes rolled past me.

'. . . Strings . . . we'll run this with the Jamaican Air in A . . .'

From the opposite direction, two violinists flew past me, clutching their precious instruments close to their bodies.

'Musicians on stage in five, please! Actors in twenty!'

We took refuge in Papa's dressing room. On his dressing table was a basket of fruit and flowers, a bottle of wine, with a label tied around the neck. He lifted the label and read it aloud.

'Welcome back to the company, Ignatius!'

He sat down at the dressing table and faced himself in the looking glass. I hoisted myself up on to the table. It looked like the shelf of an apothecary's stall, covered with jars and pots and bottles. I picked up a small, round pot from the table and sniffed its contents. It smelled like sandalwood.

Papa wiped his face with his handkerchief.

'So have you decided what to do with the ending, Papa?' I asked.

'Indeed I have.'

He began to prepare his performance mask. An array of pots of paint and little brushes nestled on the table in front of him. As he spoke, he addressed his reflection.

'You see, the problem is Iago. He uses words as poison, feeding Othello lie after lie until his mind falls sick. Othello believes that the wife who loves him, betrays him – simply because Iago says she does.'

He poured some oil from a small jug into his palms, rubbed his hands together and moved his fingers in slow circles around his cheeks. His mahogany skin gleamed under the candlelight.

'That is what leads to Othello's downfall. So how do we fix it for Othello?'

'Have him listen to some other views maybe?' I suggested.

With studied concentration, Papa painted his eyebrows with a dark powder. *Cloves*, the label read.

'Exactly, Lizzie! Desdemona speaks up in her own defence. But her words fall on stony ground. In our new version, Desdemona asserts her innocence. She speaks up and is heard. Othello listens . . .'

Papa placed six gold rings on his fingers, one by one.

'In Shakespeare's version, Emilia betrays Desdemona by giving the handkerchief to Iago. Then Iago uses the handkerchief to trap both Desdemona and Cassio with a false accusation. In our new version, Emilia refuses to give Iago the handkerchief. She speaks up, she challenges her husband, speaks out against him in public and ruins his plans.'

He stood up and spread his arms wide. 'Could you help me with my robe, Lizzie?'

I lifted the luxurious garment from the mannequin.

It was heavier than it looked. I placed it over Papa's shoulders and helped him to arrange the folds so that they fell just so.

'You see,' Papa said, 'at the beginning of the play, Othello is highly regarded by those around him. Intelligent, courageous, a charismatic leader. Our new ending does justice to Othello the man – as he could be. Not as an Elizabethan idea of an outsider.'

It sounded to me as though the solution was to listen to what the women had to say.

He picked up the medals from the dressing table and we pinned them one by one to his robe. 'Everyone has their role to play in life, Lizzie. My hope is to represent. To help change how we are seen. Expand the possibilities of who we can be . . .

'And, I have support from a dear friend,' he added, nodding towards the letter Garrick had given me last week, inviting Papa back to the stage. It was pinned up to the looking glass.

My dear friend Sancho,

I understand your desire to return to the stage post-haste!

Do not let this unfortunate accident keep you from what you were born to do.

Return to the theatre as soon as you are able and join us for a performance that audiences will never forget!

Good to meet your little girl, and her friend!

Always your friend,
Garrick

'An expression of friendship – a true treasure,' he said with a smile.

I ran my finger along the bottom edge of the paper. It was ripped, as though a strip had been torn from the bottom of the sheet.

'It's torn . . .' I observed.

'Yes, yes,' said Papa. 'But it is the message, Lizzie, not the medium that counts.'

Belle and I had arranged to meet in the stalls so that we could watch the rehearsal together. Puck had agreed to keep watch from the Tower, though of course, no chandelier was to feature in the production. From there, he said, he would have a good view of the stage and the auditorium, and he hoped to identify any threat to Papa or the other actors.

The performance began.

Once more, Roderigo and Iago prowled around the stage, plotting Othello's downfall. My skin prickled and my eyes kept darting to the balcony, to the wings, to the boxes around the auditorium. The actors seemed uneasy too, their voices quieter and their gestures more tentative as they moved nervously around the stage with none of their usual verve and fire.

I watched with bated breath, waiting only for my father's entrance.

Ash looked around for his colleague as he spoke his lines, but Papa was nowhere to be seen.

'Though in the trade of war I have slain men,

'Yet do I hold it very stuff o' th' conscience

'To do no contrived murder . . .'

The words tumbled into silence.

Belle grabbed my arm. 'Lizzie . . . when did you last see your father?'

My heart turned over in my chest.

I stood up and started down the aisle towards the stage, where the actors shifted uneasily, whispering to each other.

'Sancho? Sancho!'

Garrick calling. Greenwoode calling. Suddenly everyone was moving around, searching for my father, calling his name.

'I left him in his dressing room,' I cried, running down the corridor to Papa's room.

When I got to the door, Garrick blocked my way. His face was ashen.

Over his shoulder I could see my father slumped over his dressing table, clutching his stomach and groaning. Mary Robinson stood next to him, shaking him gently by the shoulders and calling his name. The wine bottle lay on the table in front of him, its dark red liquid spilling all over the floor.

Greenwoode appeared behind me, stopping dead when he saw the hump of my father's back.

'Lizzie!' said Garrick. 'Your father is unwell. Very unwell . . . Please go and fetch your mother, quickly! I'll send for Dr Phipps!'

As people gathered behind me, I heard their whispers as they speculated as to what had happened to Papa.

'Drunk? Poisoned? Did you see the wine bottle? Where did it come from?'

'Girls!' said Greenwoode, his face the very picture of concern. 'Take Belle's carriage! And be quick about it!'

Chapter Forty-Two

The rain beat down in sheets and we pulled up our hoods for cover. Belle's carriage waited in its usual spot. From the back we could just make out Joshua's hunched figure sitting on top, silhouetted against the darkening sky, his hood pulled down low over his head to protect him from the driving wet.

As we climbed in, Belle called out, 'To Sancho's, please, Joshua, as quickly as you can! It's an emergency!'

The carriage lurched away at speed. I grabbed the door handle to prevent myself from being thrown to the floor. My mind was full of scorpions. Could Papa really be poisoned?

'Oh Belle!' I cried. 'There was a basket of fruit on his table – from the theatre company . . . and a bottle of wine. You don't think . . .'

'Garrick said he would call for the doctor straight away,' said Belle, taking my hand. 'And your mama will know what to do.'

The carriage jostled roughly from side to side as the horses beat the ground away with their hooves. The wheels of the carriage rattled and slid in the ruts in the muddy road. Why had I even left Papa? In the heat and rush of the moment we had been sent away again, when I should have been with him!

Now I felt desperate to get to Mama.

Why was the journey taking so long?

As we turned a corner, the carriage leaned so far over to one side that we were flung to the floor.

'Joshua!' Belle cried. She rapped sharply on the carriage roof. 'Slow down, please! We want to get there quickly, but we want to get there in one piece!'

Joshua did not usually drive so recklessly, but our haste and the rain was turning our journey into a hazard. Was Joshua angry, I wondered, about having to drive us around when his work for the Sons and Daughters of Africa was so pressing?

'What is taking so long?' said Belle, pulling down the carriage window. And then, 'Where *are* we?'

I looked out of the window. Disappearing behind us, the Tower of London; off to our right, the river, the ships of

St Katharine Docks. We were heading in the wrong direction!

A wave of terror washed over me.

'Belle, we're on the other side of London! We're going the wrong way!' I beat on the roof with my fist and shouted at the top of my voice: 'Stop! Joshua, stop!'

As soon as Joshua's name left my mouth, I knew deep in my belly that something was terribly wrong. Belle took one look at my face and began to hammer on the roof with me. Together we beat and beat our fists and screamed and shouted.

'Stop! Stop the carriage now!'

We were flung violently backwards into our seats as the carriage lurched to a stop.

A sudden quiet, but for the insistent patter of the driving rain.

Outside the window, I could just make out the silhouettes of masted ships in the darkness. The docks.

We heard the driver jump down from his perch. The sound of flesh on flesh as he slapped the horses' haunches.

'There's life in you mares, I'll give you that!'

A gruff voice, dry, cracked. Definitely not Joshua. In our haste we had jumped into the carriage without more than a passing glance at the figure sitting on top holding the reins.

So who was it who had thrashed the horses to within

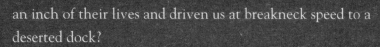

an inch of their lives and driven us at breakneck speed to a deserted dock?

Our eyes were fixed on the carriage door.

It opened to reveal a masked man in a black hat and a long, caped coat.

'So,' he snarled, his voice thick with menace. 'We've caught up with each other at last. What do you make of that, girls? My best vanishing act yet!'

Of course. It was Wilkins.

Chapter Forty-Three

43

My heart was in my throat. I swallowed hard, not wanting him to have the satisfaction of seeing my fear.

'There are people looking for us, you know,' I said, trying to keep my voice steady.

He cupped his ear, as though listening for something. 'The cavalry? No, can't hear anything. You need to hold your tongues and do exactly as you're told. No noise, no fuss, no screaming. Not a sound.'

He held a lantern aloft. It cast a ghoulish light on his face. 'Get down from the carriage and follow me.'

Even in the night air, the odour of stale tobacco clung to him. The memory of Tom's empty room flashed before me.

Broad-shouldered, Wilkins walked with a heavy stagger. We climbed down and followed behind without a sound.

The rain was no longer falling but the ground was still wet, the cobbles on the dockside oily with the residue from fishing nets. We clung to each other as we walked, trying not to slip on the stones.

I thought of my father, picturing the scene I had left him in. Mary Robinson was with him, Garrick and Greenwoode. Who would look after him now? And who might have tried to poison him?

The wind blew bitterly around us: salt, with a faint whiff of rotting fish. It was a quiet night: the only sound was the gentle lapping of water against the jetty. All along the dark river, the taverns were lighting their lamps. People, not far away, but oblivious to us and our plight.

One light flickered on and off. There was a rhythm to it, a language, as though someone was trying to communicate something. My guts felt hollow with yearning, pained with the wish that the light was flickering for us, that someone out there could see us, was thinking about us, would come for us.

'Get a move on!' growled Wilkins as he led us along the dock, past the great warehouses hulking in the darkness.

As we walked, I screwed up my eyes against the rain, trying to scan our surroundings for details that would tell me where we were, or ways out. On a corner up ahead, a sign flapped in the wind. *The Dolphin Tavern*. Behind its windows, silhouetted shadows roared and laughed drunkenly in the smoke-stained yellow light.

Around the back we trudged, into a small yard. Wilkins took a bunch of keys from his coat pocket and fumbled with them, swaying from side to side and swearing under his breath. He opened the door on to a small, dark room with two wooden pallets in the corner. On the floor beside the pallets was a tray with two tankards of water, two hunks of bread. A small barred window overlooked the dock.

'You won't be long here. But try to get away and you'll regret it.'

He swung the door closed and we heard the key turn in the lock. As his footsteps receded I tried the door, to no avail.

'What did he mean, *You won't be long here?*' I said at last.

'Maybe he means to charge a ransom for us and return us to our families?' Belle's eyes betrayed her desperate hope that Wilkins planned to send us home soon.

'We can't bank on that,' I said. 'What if he means to sell us to slave traders? To put us on a ship? We need to find a way out of this! Quickly!'

Belle looked at me imploringly. 'What do we do, Lizzie?'

It was only when I saw the fear in her eyes that I realised how afraid I truly was too.

Voices, next door.

We moved to the wall to listen.

'So where are my goods, Wilkins? You're a day late as it is.' A woman's voice. Brittle.

'I've had a change of heart. Not happy with your offer.'

'Forty pounds for two healthy girls is an incredibly generous offer.' Her voice tapped like sharp nails on glass. I'd heard it before.

'I think I could do better.'

'Don't start playing games with me, Wilkins. I've already promised them out. I've got transport arranged to take them up to Northumberland tomorrow morning. I want to get them ready. I'm not leaving here without them.'

It was Susanna Lamont! Belle's face told me that she recognised the voice as well as I did.

The sound of a chair scraping on the wooden floorboards. Wilkins' lumbering footsteps. 'Like I said. I've had a change of heart.'

'Are you threatening me, Wilkins? I wouldn't risk it. I'd have your feet swinging at Tyburn before you could say thruppence!'

'Damn your eyes, woman! You want to know the truth of it? It's too risky. Those girls know too much. About what you do, about what I do. They've written it all down. They've even been to those damned meetings. The devil knows what they've spilled already.'

The sound of a cork being pulled. A pause while he drank. He gave a loud, deep belch and went on.

'I'd rather ship them out to the West Indies. I could get a handsome rate. And I'd give you a cut.'

'I don't want a cut!' Each word was edged with steel. 'I want those girls! And don't talk to me about risk! Coming to the theatre like that in broad daylight the other day – what's wrong with you, man? You could have had us all caught and hanged!'

'I came to get my money!' Wilkins whined. 'If your friend had paid me when they were supposed to . . . I did the job they asked. *The grocer makes my life a misery*, they said! *Get rid of him*, they said! *I'll pay you handsomely*, they said! I've never seen someone so green with envy. I set it all up perfectly. Dropped the chandelier, made it look like an accident. And then they refused to pay up! I took risks –'

'They hired you to destroy Sancho, did they not? And yet Sancho still struts across the stage!'

Who were they talking about? Who would have hired someone to kill my father? I felt sick.

Miss Lamont went on. 'And anyway, I brought you your money the other day, didn't I? Sancho's girl literally ran straight into me! I thought the game was up! You're a liability!'

So *Susanna* was following Wilkins that afternoon . . .

But what about Meg?

'It's not my fault some actor decided to play the hero and save the grocer,' muttered Wilkins. 'I did what I said I would. And I took the boy off your hands into the bargain. They all think he's the one that did it. So your friend's off the hook good and proper. For now. Unless I decide to make life difficult for them. After all, they've been here. I've got proof of it.'

'I wouldn't advise it, Wilkins. We're very well connected, you know.'

'Oh, I know you two think you're above me, Miss High-and-Mighty. The pair of you are quite the double act. But I don't pretend to be anything I'm not, see? I just am what I am.'

Susanna Lamont laughed then, a hollow, ugly sound. 'Don't be ridiculous, man. You creep about in the shadows. You lurk in the dark. You're hiding just as much as we are. And you don't seem to mind Miss High-and-Mighty when my connections bring the money rolling in. You've done very well out of me so far.'

'And you've done well out of me!' Wilkins returned. 'Your friend said the best way now to stop the grocer was to take the girls. And I've done that. They're out of your way. Those girls wouldn't be even be next door right now if it weren't for me.'

Who did he mean? Would someone at the theatre really have handed us over to someone like Wilkins? Did someone there really have so much hatred for my father?

'And now it's time to hand them over as we agreed,' said Miss Lamont.

'Well it's too late, woman. I've already made the sale. You'll have to put your buyer off and find another deal. Now, if you'll excuse me . . .'

The sound of the door opening.

'I've got a ship to load up.'

Chapter Forty-Four

W as I surprised to discover that Susanna Lamont had had a hand in this horrible affair? Not particularly. Belle and I had both felt a creeping unease during our meeting with her at the Jamaica Coffee House, but had not been able to articulate why. A memory flashed before me – her dog, with an oval-shaped locket around its neck. In my mind's eye I saw once more her saccharine smile as she disappeared through the door marked 'Auction Room'.

Was it really people who were being auctioned off in that dreadful place?

We had to get out of here. Our time was running out.

'Belle, we've got to go!' I hissed. 'You heard him say he was loading up a ship . . .'

'But how?' said Belle.

I stared out of the tiny window that overlooked the dock,

racking my brains for a way out. Once more, the little light across the water flickered in three short bursts. I waited and watched. They came again. Three short flashes of light. An idea began to take shape in my mind.

'Maybe we can't get out of here ourselves right now, with Wilkins watching over us,' I said. 'But what if we can convince Wilkins that *he* needs to escape?'

'What do you mean?' Belle's voice was pinched with anxiety.

'I mean, persuade him that he is being watched, and that a wrong move would mean the end for him.'

'But how, Lizzie? No one knows we're here. No one's coming!'

'Remember in the tunnel?' I said. 'The conversation between your uncle and my father? Your uncle is one of the most powerful men in the land. I've been thinking about all the things Papa said to him that afternoon. Who knows, maybe Wilkins even heard him too. And the Sons and Daughters of Africa meeting. We know that they're planning a rescue raid. The only thing holding them back was the location. They didn't know where Wilkins was keeping everyone. If we can convince him that they *do* know where he is . . .'

Belle shook her head. 'I don't know, Lizzie –'

'We've got to try!' I said. 'Think of it as another

performance. Just follow my lead. If this goes according to plan, Wilkins will be out of here in a trice. All we have to do now is wait for him to come in.'

After moments that felt like hours, the key sounded in the lock. Wilkins' hulking frame filled the doorway. In one hand, he held a whisky bottle; in the other, a heavy iron chain. He swayed, an axed tree about to fall.

'Up you get,' he said. 'Time to go!'

I drew myself up to my full height and squared my shoulders.

'Are you sure you really want to walk us out of here?' I said.

He laughed. 'A smart one, are we?' He stepped towards me and lowered over me. 'Do as I say,' he muttered through gritted teeth.

'I'm serious, Wilkins,' I said. 'You may have stolen our notes, but do you really think we've kept quiet about what we know? We've shared all our information with Lord Mansfield. So have the Sons and Daughters of Africa. Everyone knows what you're up to, and they've been on your trail for days.'

'Stop jabbering and follow me!' Wilkins bellowed.

'You can try and scare us,' I said. 'I don't care. Everything you do right now is being watched. If you do anything to hurt us now, you'll be executed at Tyburn for sure.'

He narrowed his eyes at me, then flicked his gaze towards the door. 'What do you mean, being watched?'

'I told you, but you didn't believe me!' I said with a shrug. 'Do you really think Lord Mansfield would stand by and let you put us on a slave ship? There's a regiment out there just waiting for the word. Look outside!'

He glanced towards the window, took a step towards the door.

'At the signal, they'll be all over this place,' I continued. 'And you, my friend, you'll be lucky to even make it to Bow Street. Kidnapping, trafficking, attempted murder. If you lay a hand on *either* of us, if you harm us in any way, Mansfield won't hold back.'

'You've tried that one with me already, Missy.' Wilkins was slurring now. 'Like I said, I don't hear the sound of hooves.'

'They're not galloping, Wilkins,' I said. 'They're watching. Waiting for you to put a foot wrong so they can really have you. Mansfield has men lined up all the way along the bank of the river. They've been signalling to us and to each other since we've been here.' I took a deep breath. 'I've never felt safer in my life.'

'What do you mean!' he roared, drawing a wild arc in the air with the empty whisky bottle as he spun around to follow my gaze to the window. Whisky splashed on to the floor at his feet.

'Oh, they're out there, Wilkins.' I heard my voice grow in confidence. 'Haven't you seen their lights? Three flashes to say they have you in sight. Five to tell the guards on this side of the river to move in. The Sons and Daughters of Africa have been following you for days. They saw you above the stage, they saw you outside our shop the following night, they saw you back at the theatre the other day. They've been tailing you all along. My father put them in touch with Lord Mansfield. He's called together a regiment to bring you in.'

'So why haven't they arrested me then?' Wilkins snarled, his lips pulling back over his teeth, like a wolf's.

'Because they need to catch you in the act,' I explained. 'This is the first time they've caught up with you when you've actually had people in tow. This is the one that will ensure your arrest. It's up to you. You can take your chances and slip away now, or you can carry on with your plan under the eye of the law. They'll have Lamont by now.'

His eyes popped. 'What!'

'Oh yes they know all about Lamont,' I said. 'Didn't you realise? She'll no doubt be spilling the beans already. Or did you think perhaps she would . . . *protect* you if they caught up with her? Don't you know what she means when she talks about friends in high places?'

He reeled, as though I had pushed him. 'Those damn . . . I knew they couldn't be trusted! I knew it!'

He glared out of the window again. Belle crouched in the corner, her eyes glued to Wilkins. I watched the shore, breath held, waiting, willing those lights to fire up again. Any time now. It had to be, any time now.

There! There it was again. One. Two. Three! Perfect!

Wilkins staggered backwards.

Belle stood up. Her voice, when it came, was strong and steady.

'I can guarantee you, Mr Wilkins, if any harm comes to either of us, if you even so much as take another step towards us – Lord Mansfield will see you hanged before daybreak.'

She pushed her chin upwards and held him with her eyes, unflinching.

Wilkins looked as though the air had been punched out of him. He stared around in wild horror before flinging open the door and bolting from the room as though a thousand devils were after him. Seconds later, we heard the sound of horse hooves beating away the ground. Wilkins had fled.

We waited as the sound disappeared into the distance.

Belle put her hands to her face. 'It can't be true! Has he really just gone and left us?'

I sank back against the wall and closed my eyes for a moment.

'Of course he has, Belle. He's a bully and a coward. Lamont rattled his cage. All we had to was open it!'

Chapter Forty-Five

We decided to ransack Wilkins' office for every shred of evidence we could find before heading home. We did not want to come this far only to have him slip though our fingers for lack of proof.

We crept out on to the dock, and into the warehouse next door. Wilkins hadn't even bothered to close the door. Lamont was right. He was a liability.

Inside, row upon row of barrels were stacked around the edges of the room. Rats squeaked and scratched in the cobwebbed corners.

In the centre, a large table. Amidst the empty whisky bottles were countless piles of papers. Every written document we could find, we collected. I rifled through them and found receipts, ledgers, bills of sale. Lists of names and ages: people, many of them children, sold as though they were objects.

Sold to the highest bidders, then sent by coach to country estates, to work for no pay, as decoration, as status symbols. Others sent off to sugar plantations in the West Indies.

Scipio, aged nine. Rosetta, aged fourteen. Neptune, aged eleven. Mercury, aged twelve. Mercury! A flash of hope, perhaps, that he would be found?

Letters and contracts between Wilkins and Lamont. For some, there was no sense of shame in trading in human beings. As a result, there was a solid paper trail: evidence everywhere.

'Lizzie,' Belle said quietly. 'Wilkins kept referring to a friend of Susanna Lamont's at the theatre. Who do you think he meant?'

I thought of the letter I had seen on Papa's looking glass. Torn along the bottom edge, as though someone had ripped away a strip for some other purpose. To write an address . . .

I didn't even want to say the name that tugged in my mind like a stitch in a wound.

The very person who had seemed to be the kindest friend to Papa all along, who had urged him repeatedly to return to the theatre? The man that Papa trusted above everyone else in the company?

Could it really be Garrick? Papa would be utterly devastated.

I shook my head, unable to speak. Belle nodded her understanding.

I opened the last drawer in Wilkins' desk. There was Belle's leather pouch. I pulled it out and opened it up.

'Our case notes!'

All of our interview notes, all of Belle's work, exactly as we had recorded it, was still safe in the pouch.

That was it. We had what we needed.

All the paper we had gathered, we placed in the pouch alongside our notes.

As I went to close the drawer, I noticed a paper envelope, pushed to the back. I pulled it out: inside, a handkerchief, neatly folded. White cotton, handstitched with a border of dark green trees around its edge. In the corner, Madame Hassan's trademark. Had this handkerchief, like Papa's, been made especially for its owner, with a motif symbolic of their name? What was Wilkins' first name, I wondered? Each tree had a narrow trunk and a round crown of foliage. What kind of tree was it?

I slid the handkerchief into the pouch along with our case notes.

'Look!' said Belle, holding up a huge ring of iron keys. 'I think we should take these.'

'Right,' I said, casting one final glance around the room where so many grim exchanges had been agreed. 'Then let's get out of here.'

Chapter Forty-Six

A s we emerged from Wilkins' yard, the sun cast a reddish glow over the docks, illuminating the ships and warehouses. A giant galleon cast a forbidding silhouette against the sky, its sails billowing in the chilly dawn breeze. It seemed to groan as it rocked and creaked in the dock.

The *Apollo*.

The sight of it filled me with a dread I had never known. We had to get away from there. I looked around, trying to get my bearings. We would have to head west to get back home. I would need to use the position of the sun, the bends in the river and the landmarks on the skyline to guide me.

Belle cocked her head, listening intently to a sound I had not heard.

'Do you hear that, Lizzie?' she said.

A knocking, coming from inside one of the warehouses.

Belle approached and tried the door. It was locked. Sounds of a muffled voice from within, someone in distress.

'Lizzie, quick!' Belle said. 'The keys!'

I passed her the giant ring of keys and she fumbled with them in haste, trying each one in turn. Finally, one twisted. Belle pushed the large door open to reveal a young man, sitting in the corner of the warehouse, hands tied behind his back, his breath coming in short, rapid gasps.

Tom!

'Help me to get him up!' I said to Belle.

Gently we moved him into a sitting position against the wall. His eyes were closed and his head lolled back, mouth open. Beside him on the floor was a tankard of water. I brought it to his lips. He spluttered, then drank, blinking as he revived. He took a breath to speak and coughed then, hard, his chest rattling with the force of it. He tried again.

'Lizzie! I heard your voice . . . didn't know if I was dreaming . . .We need to leave . . . before he comes back.'

The sudden sound of horses' hooves on the cobbles sent Tom scuttling back against the wall. 'Wilkins!' he whispered.

I grabbed a plank of wood from the ground next to Tom, took a step towards the door and braced myself.

The door swung open slowly.

Wilkins was nowhere to be seen.

Standing before us, hands on hips, was Meg.

'Lizzie Sancho. You're a difficult girl to find!' she declared.

Meg! How could I have forgotten about her? Had Wilkins sent her after us?

'And you must be Belle,' she said, a tiger again.

I jabbed the air with the plank of wood. 'Don't. Come. Any. Closer!'

She raised her eyebrows and held up her hands. 'I'm impressed, girl. You got guts, that's for sure. But I know you got smarts too. And you're not using your smarts right now.'

I faltered. What was she talking about?

'Whose side do you think I'm on, girl? Get real, now!'

Meg placed a fist over her chest.

My hands began to shake.

'I'm your rescue party, sister! Though I have to admit,' she said, glancing round the room, 'you haven't done too badly without me!'

I dropped the plank to the ground. Tears of relief pricked my eyes. 'So you're . . .'

'A Daughter of Africa, yes. I've been tracking Wilkins undercover. Have to say you haven't made life easy for me, though,' Meg said, kneeling down beside Tom. 'Chasing around after him in broad daylight and the like. But I admire your courage.'

She produced a large knife from her back pocket.

Its blade glinted in the burning dawn light. Tom covered his head with his arms, his eyes wide with fear.

'It's all right, Tom. I'm certainly not going to hurt you,' Meg said. 'Never used a knife on flesh in my life. Let's get these ropes off you.'

Her voice was the gentlest I had heard it. She cut the ropes from Tom's wrists and placed the knife back in its sheath. She reached into her cloak, brought out a small dark phial of liquid and removed the stopper with her teeth. She poured out a deep amber liquid into her palm and massaged it gently into the wounds on Tom's wrists. From a trouser pocket, she produced a hip flask, unscrewed the cap and lifted it to Tom's lips.

'You need food,' she said, holding the back of Tom's head while he drank. 'Let's get you over to the Guinea Coffee House. You'll be met there and looked after. We've got people down at the dock, ready to ambush the *Apollo*. But we need to move quickly.'

Outside, three centaurs seemed to emerge from the early morning mist. Was I dreaming? I was exhausted, that was for certain. Two women and a man, on horseback, riding slowly towards us, silhouetted by a fiery dawn.

'Lizzie, meet Juno, Adah and Ezekiel,' said Meg. 'Belle, climb up there with Juno. Tom, you ride with Ezekiel. Lizzie, you can come with me on Sagitarr. Adah here is our security for the journey.'

Sagitarr was a chestnut-brown stallion, nodding and stamping the ground with its heavy hooves. I had never been on a horse, but I reckoned there was a first time for everything. Meg climbed on and pulled me up behind her. Relief washed over me like dawn sunlight as I locked my arms around her waist and we started the long journey home.

As the sun rose, London looked more magnificent than ever. We galloped through the fields in the east, along the north bank of the Thames. Ahead of us the dome of St Paul's glowed golden under the burning sky. Did London always look this beautiful in the dawn light, or were these rosy visions of my city all the more powerful because I had believed that perhaps I would never see them again?

The horses slowed as we entered the city. Gaggles of women and men tumbled out of taverns or lolled in doorways. Snatches of song drifted into the air, mingled with the mist that rose up from the river.

'My father, Meg!' I gasped suddenly. 'Is he all right? He was unwell . . .'

'You've no need to worry about him,' Meg said. 'He's

safe and sound at home with your mother. That wine was poisoned, but Dr Phipps got to him in time. Your father's a survivor, no doubt about it.'

We turned up Chancery Lane, where wigged lawyers and their young clerks were beginning to make their way to the Inns of Court, before finally riding into Drury Lane. I felt a chill as we passed the theatre.

'Is Joshua all right?' called Belle sleepily from the horse beside us, where she sat behind Juno. 'Wilkins took the carriage!'

'Wilkins ambushed him while you were in the theatre,' Meg said. 'Knocked him out and left him in a back street. Two women found him and helped him to the nearest tavern. We've got people all over the city who are sympathetic to our cause. It was Joshua who let us know to come after you. He's back at the Guinea Coffee House and he's safe.'

How could we have jumped into that carriage like that? An act of carelessness I would not be repeating.

'It's a collective effort between us all,' Meg went on. 'Joshua knows the city inside out. He takes messages across town for us. When brothers and sisters land here from the Caribbean, he gets them settled, makes sure they know who we are, how to find us if they need help.

'Your father writes up our pamphlets and your mother has them printed for us. Frances goes out on to the streets to deliver them and recruit new members. I work at the theatres selling playbills, so I hand out pamphlets at the same time. It's all about spreading the word.'

The woman selling playbills at the theatre! That was how she knew who I was!

'So was it you that took in the delivery of oranges the day I was watching the stage door?' I said.

We turned into the Strand, steering in between the wagons taking goods from the riverside and making their way up towards the market. Meg cast an arch look back over her shoulder.

'So you were watching the stage door?' she said. 'I get it now. I took the oranges down to the theatre kitchen. That's when Wilkins turned up at the theatre to confront his accomplices and demand his money. I missed his arrival, I missed the meeting. By the time I got back, he was leaving. With you behind him! You gave me a run for my money, girl!'

So Meg *had* been chasing after me, in a sense – but to keep me safe from Wilkins.

We were back in Westminster. Meg pulled our horse to a stop outside the shop.

'You certainly don't need to worry about Wilkins any more,' she said. 'We intercepted him on the road east out of the docks. Our people took him straight to Bow Street.

It's all arranged. It's his accomplices we need to unveil now. I'm going to set you down here. I'll take Tom to the Guinea and get Belle back home.

'I've got an appointment with Mansfield.'

ACT V

Chapter Forty-Seven

*'The play's the thing
Wherein I'll catch the conscience of the king!'
Hamlet, Act II, Scene 2*

Tonight was set for the opening night of *Othello*. Now there was only one piece of the puzzle missing. Only one co-conspirator left to unveil.

Belle and I had drawn together our final plans by letter.

Friday 25th April

Dear Belle,

So Wilkins is in jail, but Lamont still walks free and will take the stage alongside Papa tonight. I am terrified that she and the third conspirator will make another attempt on Papa's life unless we can unveil them. If we want to finish this properly, we have to reveal their identity in public. We must name and shame all three.

The scrap of paper bearing Tom's address fits perfectly with the page on which Garrick wrote his letter to Papa. One piece clearly torn from the other. That clue points without question to Garrick, no?

Lizzie

Dear Lizzie,

I agree that the letter and the address point to Garrick, but then what is his motive? And why would he poison your father, then call the doctor to save him?

Wilkins mentioned envy in his conversation with Lamont. Something doesn't add up. I went back to the notes from our interview with Ash about motive.

I think we should keep looking.

Belle

Dear Belle,

I am looking at the handkerchief that I found in Wilkins' office at the dockyard, with its border of trees around the edge. If this is one of Madame Hassan's handkerchiefs, the pattern represents the name of the owner! I thought that maybe the trees signalled Wilkins' first name. But the documents we took from his office reveal his first name as John.

So the handkerchief must belong to someone else.

I made a list of first names of people at the theatre it could belong to:

- Mary
- Susanna
- David
- Dominic
- William
- Tom
- Puck

None of them seem to have any relation to trees whatsoever – unless you can tell me different?

Here is a drawing of what one of the trees looks like:

Yours,
Lizzie

Dear Lizzie,

I have consulted a book of the trees of England and made a list of names of trees, yet I cannot establish a connection with any of the first names of the people from the theatre?

Is it lack of sleep that prevents us from seeing what we are missing?

Yours,
Belle

Dear Belle,

How could I have missed what has been staring me in the face?

The handkerchief is indeed the final clue.

It's not a first name the trees represent.

It's a surname.

We've got him.

Lizzie

Chapter Forty-Eight

I had managed to persuade Papa that he should go ahead with the performance and asked if he would allow Belle and me some time with the audience to reveal the conspirators and their plot. I did not share my suspicions, but begged him to trust me. Meg had shared with my parents the discoveries that Belle and I had made so far. They were shocked, disconcerted, but ultimately willingly to let us finish the job, on the condition that Meg and her comrades were on hand.

Meg had taken the documents proving the collaboration between Wilkins and Lamont and their slave-trading deals. She had passed them directly to Lord Mansfield. Wilkins had been arrested and was at Newgate. Belle had spoken to her uncle to persuade him of Tom's innocence and convince him to let us finish what we had started.

Papa was hesitant. Mama said she thought it sounded dangerous – what if they tried to strike again? – but I reassured them that it was all carefully arranged. We had many comrades onside and this was our final chance to put a stop to the attempts on Papa's life.

'This horrible business has been conducted behind the scenes, in the shadows!' I explained. 'It's time for people to see and hear what has really been going on, right under their noses!'

So Papa finally agreed that I should take up a box in the auditorium with Mama, Frances, Mary, Kitty and Billy. From there, I would tell the story from the beginning.

Opposite me, in her family box on the other side of the theatre, was Belle, with her aunt and uncle, and Joshua. Lord Mansfield raised a hand and nodded. At the edges of the stalls stood the chief constable of Bow Street, with two of his men.

Garrick and Greenwoode sat in the front row, closest to the stage. Both looked nervous.

Puck and Tom were stationed backstage, keeping watch from the wings. With them, Meg and George. In the upper gallery, Juno, Adah, Ezekiel and Brother Ottobah Cugoano sat with other members of the Sons and Daughters of Africa and customers from the tea shop, eyes firmly fixed on the stage.

The buzz in the crowd was undeniable. People had dressed up in their finest: every row was packed with dresses and frockcoats in crimson, magenta, emerald, ochre. Some, enthused by the play's setting, wore Venetian masks. Little clusters of smaller chandeliers lit the auditorium and the stage, the candles giving off a softer light for a mysterious atmosphere. The theatre had never looked more splendid.

Garrick stood to introduce the production and the audience settled into a reverent hush.

'Ladies and gentlemen!' he declared. 'Welcome to the Theatre Royal, Drury Lane, and this most extraordinary opening night. It gives me immense pleasure to welcome our good friend Ignatius Sancho back to the stage, to play the role he was born to – Othello. Before we begin, a few words from Ignatius!'

Papa strode on to the stage in his red cloak, hands upraised for the applause that accompanied him.

'Good evening, friends and comrades,' he said. 'I would like to invite some colleagues to the stage to join Mr Garrick and myself for a prelude to our performance: Miss Susanna Lamont, Mr William Ash, Tom Johnson, Puck Pathak and Dominic Greenwoode.'

Susanna Lamont stepped out of the wings, looking furtively around her. Meg and George appeared either side of her, blocking any chance of a swift exit. She snapped open a fan and beat it in tiny flutters in front of her face.

Tom and Puck stepped on to the stage together. Tom caught my eye and I nodded to reassure him.

Ash strode up to Papa and shook his hand. Greenwoode hovered at the edge of the stage, his arms crossed, his brow furrowed.

'Before we proceed,' said Papa. 'I must let you know that while we have been playing out *The Tragedy of Othello*, a far deeper tragedy has been playing out offstage.'

An awed hush fell over the room.

Susanna glanced sideways at Meg. Her face was a mask of cool defiance, but her fan waved back and forth in furious agitation.

Papa raised his arm towards where I was seated in the box with Mama.

'It is only right you should hear this from the people to whom we owe this special evening. May I present . . . my daughter Lizzie Sancho, and Miss Dido Belle.'

All eyes turned towards me. I stood slowly, my legs wobbling, my voice threatening to falter. But I remembered what Papa had always taught me. If you are given the platform and the space to speak out – use it well.

I cleared my throat, and looked at the cast, assembled on the stage. I looked out at the sea of faces in the auditorium, and across the theatre at Belle. For a moment I was transported to that opening night two weeks ago, when we had first met, when the chandelier had come crashing to the stage. So much had happened since then.

Belle pushed up on to her feet and nodded at me. It was time.

I wiped my hot palms on my breeches and took a deep breath.

'As you all know, my father is about to take the stage to perform the role of Othello. But we have discovered a plot to destroy my father and sabotage a production daring enough to put a Black man centre stage,' I continued. 'And the conspirators are steeped in the most shameful business our society knows.'

Murmurings and questions rippled through the crowd. I glanced at Mama for support. She nodded back.

'The conspirators would have you believe that a young man named Tom dropped a chandelier to the stage on opening night,' I said, more steadily now. 'The chandelier that nearly crushed my father.'

At this, Papa looked up at me and placed a hand on his chest. Mama clutched Kitty and Billy closer to her on her lap.

I continued. 'They even planted stories in the newspaper suggesting that he had guiltily fled the scene.'

'I didn't do that!' called Tom suddenly from the edge of the stage. 'I would never have done that,' he added, looking earnestly at Papa.

'We know, Tom,' Papa replied gently. 'And I never doubted you.'

I turned back to the audience. 'But those same conspirators paid someone to seize Tom from his home that evening. A bounty hunter!'

I held up the poster of Wilkins and Belle took up the story.

'John Wilkins!' she announced. All eyes swept up to her. 'We had thought we would all be safer after my uncle's Somerset ruling, but this man kidnapped Tom and locked him up at the docks, hoping to sell him to the captain of a slaving ship called the *Apollo*, bound for Barbados. He kidnapped us too, when he knew we were getting close to the truth.'

A distinct ripple of unease worked its way around the crowd.

Mary Robinson stepped forward, her hand raised.

'If Wilkins is a bounty hunter, why did he try to kill Ignatius?' she said. 'Why not kidnap him like he did the others?'

'We wondered the same, Miss Robinson,' I said. 'Bounty hunters are motivated by money. Wilkins was prepared to do all manner of horrible things to earn it. He tried to kill my father simply because someone – someone here among us – paid him to do so.'

The auditorium began to buzz with murmurs of speculation.

'The motivation of the person who wanted my father dead was pure envy. That was the key to understanding who was behind all this. When Garrick and my father became friends, this person was racked with envy. He saw himself as Garrick's next bright star. He had hopes of playing leading roles: Romeo, Hamlet! But it was not to be – was it, Mr Greenwoode?'

A collective gasp of horror went up from the audience.

Greenwoode's face had turned a livid white.

'What a preposterous suggestion!' he snarled. He stared about him wildly. 'Surely you're not going to take the word of two *little girls* against that of a grown man!'

Papa was shaking his head in disbelief. Mary helped him to a chair in the corner of the stage and he sank into it.

Garrick was staring, horrified, at Greenwoode. He opened his mouth but no sound came out.

I went on. 'This man paid Wilkins to drop the chandelier on to the stage with the intention of killing my father. When Mr Ash saved Papa, Greenwoode needed to change tack. His plan had been foiled. So he pretended that he was worried for my father, kept insisting that it was not safe for him to return to the stage. Anything to keep him away from the theatre, anything to keep him from rising to stardom on the stage he felt was his.'

'He even approached my uncle and tried to persuade him to cancel the production,' added Belle. 'And all along, we thought he was acting out of concern for Mr Sancho's safety. But in fact he was simply desperate to stop the production of *Othello* from going ahead.'

Garrick faced Greenwoode directly. 'Greenwoode!' he demanded. 'Is this true?'

Greenwoode wore the haggard expression of a wounded wolf, caught in a trap.

Garrick spread his arms wide. 'But why go to such lengths? Why put Sancho in such terrible danger? And how, Greenwoode, how could you have involved yourself with the shameful business of slave trading?'

Greenwoode cast a disdainful look in my direction. 'I'm sure these *little girls* would be happy to fill you in,' he hissed. 'If they're as clever as they think they are!'

'Perhaps,' I said in my loudest voice, 'we should hear from your accomplice on that point. A professional slave trader, working in the theatre as an actress. Susanna Lamont!'

Some of the women in the audience gasped. Others, who had been accompanied to the theatre by their servants, remained tellingly silent. Lamont folded away her fan and looked daggers at me, but I was not afraid.

'Miss Lamont sensed Greenwoode's hatred of my father, and she fed it. She told him she knew someone who could solve his "problem" for him. Wilkins. They've been working closely together for years. Lamont calls herself a "collector". But the truth of it is, she buys and sells people. She employs bounty hunters to kidnap young people, and she auctions them off to country estates or plantations in the West Indies. People come to her when they want an enslaved servant, no questions asked.'

I thought of Mercury and my voice wedged in my throat for a moment.

A roar of dismay reverberated around the theatre.

'Spare me your outrage!' Lamont hissed at the crowd. She scanned the balconies as she spoke. 'I've seen *you* out walking with your Black companion at your side. And I know where the money came from to pay for the grand house *you* own on the Square!'

Fans went up in front of faces. A couple of people left their seats and started to make their way towards the exit. The theatre was becoming noisier and more and more unsettled.

'Who are you to judge me?' Lamont challenged. 'A woman has to make a living!'

'For shame!' cried Mama, standing up suddenly. Around her, the cry echoed and repeated – 'For shame! For shame!'

Frances laid her hand gently on Mama's arm, and she took her seat without taking her eyes off Lamont.

I picked up the story again.

'Greenwoode hired Wilkins to kill my father. He gave him Tom's address so that Wilkins could stop Tom from coming to the theatre on opening night, take his place in the Tower and drop the chandelier. Thanks to Mr Ash's lightning reactions, Papa survived. But Wilkins – greedy as ever – saw an opportunity to double his money by kidnapping and selling Tom. Tom's disappearance could be used to suggest that he was the one who had dropped the chandelier. One crime would help to draw a veil over the other.'

Greenwoode's brows were drawn together in fury.

'I was so confused when I realised that the address had been torn from the paper that Garrick used to write a letter to my father. I couldn't believe that Garrick was the man we were looking for. But of course, it was Greenwoode who had carelessly left the torn sheet in Garrick's paper drawer.'

Garrick looked pale as the moon, his face wracked with disappointment and betrayal.

Puck stepped forward and put his hand on Tom's shoulder. 'I thought I'd never see my friend again,' he said. 'We went to his house to try and find him a couple of days after the incident. He was nowhere to be seen. I told Miss

Lamont all about it because I thought she would help us. She had always seemed so . . .' He shot her a piercing look. 'So . . . kind.'

Susanna Lamont tossed her head dismissively. She wore a sneer of utter contempt.

'You're right, Puck,' I rejoined from the box where I stood. 'Lamont's a professional actress. She had us fooled for a while, too. But no one can hide such a cold heart for long. She kept revealing flashes of cruelty. She even gave Mercury's precious locket to her dog to wear!'

I turned to face the balcony where Juno and Adah, Ottobah and Ezekiel sat, watching me intently.

'It started to fall into place when we happened on a meeting of the Sons and Daughters of Africa,' I said. 'That's how we found out about the Vanishings. And that's how we discovered who Wilkins really was. We owe a great debt to them – our lives, even – and I thank them for it. Meg, Adah, Joshua, Brother Ottobah, my sister Frances and all their comrades. They are the people who have been rescuing brothers and sisters from the likes of Lamont and Wilkins for months now.'

Our friends placed their fists over their hearts as I had seen Papa do.

Belle spoke up next.

'But as Greenwoode became more and more desperate

to destroy Mr Sancho, Wilkins and Lamont upped their stakes and decided to come after us,' she said. 'Greenwoode poisoned Mr Sancho, Wilkins ambushed Joshua, seized us and drove us out to the docks. We overheard Lamont and Wilkins – an ugly conversation if ever I heard one. It was soon clear how little loyalty there was between them. We used this to engineer a ruse to convince Wilkins that he was on the verge of capture. When he ran away and left us, we ransacked his office.'

Belle held up her leather pouch.

'We found all the notes we had been keeping on the case, stolen by Wilkins, and all the paperwork relating to the Vanishings. The lack of shame over the slave trade has produced a mountain of evidence . . .'

She handed the pouch to Lord Mansfield, who nodded his respect to her, his eyes shining with pride.

'That's when we found the final piece of the puzzle – the handkerchief,' Belle continued. 'Wilkins told Lamont that he had evidence of her accomplice's visit to the docks. That they had left something behind that would identify them. Lizzie recognised the work in the handkerchief immediately because she had had one made for her father, by Madame Hassan at Maiden Lane.'

Mama handed me my father's handkerchief and I held it up to the light.

'You see, on my father's handkerchief, the flames symbolise his name, Ignatius,' I concluded. 'But on this one, the one we found in Wilkins' office, this border of trees . . . The handkerchief belongs to Greenwoode.'

Chapter Forty-Nine

My father got up and walked to the front of the stage. The audience seemed to be holding their breath.

'Thank you, Lizzie. Thank you, Belle.' He held up an arm towards each of us. 'You have been determined, from the beginning, to right the wrong you saw playing out in front of you. And you have shown great courage in doing so.'

Lord Mansfield got to his feet.

'Hear hear, Sancho!' he declared. 'Our men are ready to take Lamont and Greenwoode down to Newgate to take their confessions. Wilkins is, as you know, already there. No one is in any doubt as to the depths of their guilt.'

'And what of us, Garrick?' shouted Greenwoode, as two uniformed men grabbed him by the arms and ushered him towards the exit. 'It was always us! A golden partnership!

I waited patiently for my moment in the spotlight, didn't I? Soon, you said. One day soon. And then Sancho came along. And suddenly you'd cast him in a lead role.'

He turned and narrowed his eyes at my father. 'He isn't – he isn't even one of us!'

At this, shouts of consternation went up from the balcony and the Sons and Daughters began to push up on to their feet. I felt sick.

Papa stepped forward, the very model of calm. 'Not one of *you*?' he whispered. 'Not one of *you*, you say Greenwoode?

'And yet, for almost fifty years now have I lived in this country, laboured in this country, and given service at every level. I have fetched and carried, cooked and cleaned for those too idle to do so for themselves. I have married here, raised children here, built a business here, voted here. I have given you music to dance to, and literature to light your evenings by the fire. And I have done so with joy! This is my home as much as it is yours, Greenwoode. It is my wife's home, my children's home – we belong here.

'If, however, by *us*, you mean those who are willing to buy and sell people for profit, or those who would snatch children away from their families and friends, or those who are so consumed by their own jealousy that they are driven to the murky depths of murder, then, yes, by those standards, Greenwoode, I can proudly say, that I am *not* one of *you*.'

Silence fell around the theatre like a soft velvet curtain.

'And now, if you will excuse us, we have a play to perform,' said Papa.

Greenwoode and Lamont were ushered out of the room. Beside me, Mama stood up and began to clap. Frances and Mary joined her, Kitty and Billy too. Lord and Lady Mansfield stood and applauded, nodding silently at my mother as they did so. The Sons and Daughters of Africa stood side by side, their fists placed over the chests, heads bowed.

Throughout the auditorium, brothers and sisters pushed on to their feet one by one, clapping. Row by row, the rest of the audience followed, standing side by side, saying with the beat of their hands together what there were no more words to express.

Chapter Fifty

The London Chronicle

Three suspects appeared in court today charged with kidnapping and attempted murder. Susanna Lamont (25), John Wilkins (46) and Dominic Greenwoode (34), were all involved in recent events at the Theatre Royal, Drury Lane. All three will be imprisoned at Newgate indefinitely.

Lamont and Wilkins have written lengthy confessions giving details of the extent of their crimes. But when questioned, Dominic Greenwoode merely said:

'Demand me nothing. What you know you know. From this time forth I never will speak word.'

STAGE DOOR MAGAZINE

Othello returns triumphant!

Following a devastating series of events and revelations at the Theatre Royal, Drury Lane, David Garrick's stunning new production of *Othello* – in a radical re-write by actor Ignatius Sancho – opened to a packed house.

In an intriguing new take on the famous tragedy by William Shakespeare, the women of the play, Desdemona (an outstanding performance by Mary Robinson) and Emilia (an assured debut from Ann Sancho) speak up and speak out. In doing so, they change the course of events and wrestle back control of the plot from the machinations of the villain Iago.

This writer does not wish to give anything away regarding the intricacies of the new plot, but suffice to say, audiences will not be disappointed by the play's new ending.

In an exclusive interview for *Stage Door*, lead actor Ignatius Sancho, who worked closely with the female cast members and with his Director David Garrick to produce a more nuanced characterisation of *Othello*, told us:

'What we need is to write our own plays, our own

poetry, our own novels. Think of all the stories we could tell. Our tragedies, yes, of course. But our comedies too. Our joys, our magic, our power. Stories about our families, stories about our loves, about our passions, our talents, our dreams, our challenges . . . Think, people, what a wonder that would be. The written word gives us life into the future. Invites us to speak to those not yet born.

'Imagine, people, imagine!'

L & B

Turn to pages 10–12 for more exclusive interviews
with the cast and crew.

Papa's new version of *Othello* ran for fifteen weeks at Drury Lane, playing to packed houses every night and garnering exuberant reviews. Garrick was elated.

'A most fitting note on which to end what has been a most illuminating and rewarding career!' he declared.

Papa was the happiest I had seen him yet. The play drew more and more customers to the shop: people eager to discuss the re-write and what it meant for would-be actors. The writers' salon thrived: Papa spent his mornings running workshops for young hopefuls wishing to hone their craft and create brilliant new stories for performance or publication.

Mama invested some of the profits from the show into setting up a small school in the shop on Saturday mornings, with a focus on teaching African history and culture, and 'skills in the business of life'.

The Sons and Daughters of Africa continued to rally and resist on all fronts, led by Captain Margaret Ebunolorum – or, as we knew her, Meg – and ably assisted by Brother Ezekiel.

Brother Ottobah Cugoano continued to speak publicly and would later write and publish his searing political tract, *Thoughts and Sentiments on the Evil of Slavery*.

Joshua Jones continued with his studies in law so that he could help people arriving in the city for the first time to find safe housing, gainful employment and education. I asked Frances if she and Joshua were officially stepping out together, but she told me in no uncertain terms to mind my own business.

Mercury, however, was still missing. Lord Mansfield had sent guards out to a number of addresses to try and retrieve him, but he had not yet been found. My heart ached every day for him.

'We'll find him, Lizzie,' Mama told me, when I showed her a new poster that had been made about his disappearance all those months ago. 'We will find him.'

When the show closed, the Mansfields hosted a wrap party to celebrate its success. A masquerade ball in the grounds of Kenwood House.

We arrived bedecked in matching family outfits of gold satin, with masks made by Madame Hassan to make us look like a pride of lions.

Kenwood looked dazzling.

Strings of lanterns in the trees cast myriad blooms of coloured light around the pond. Beams of white moonlight lit up groups of masked revellers as they played hide-and-seek among the trees, their satin gowns and cloaks sweeping behind them as they darted in and out of the shadows. Acrobats tumbled and flew, lithe and agile in their black-and-white harlequined costumes.

Will, Sally, George and Mary played minuets and reels to a whooping, shouting crowd who danced in circles around the band. Peals of laughter blended with silver notes of jubilant music – together they floated up into the night sky.

When we arrived, Belle welcomed us into the house, resplendent in a scarlet satin cape and dress. Everyone stood, spellbound for a moment, as they took in the imposing grandeur of the hall.

'Come in, come in!' said Belle. 'They're about to unveil the portrait!'

The highlight of the evening was to be the unveiling of a group portrait in the library that the Mansfields had commissioned to mark the beginning of a relationship between our two families. Belle and I stood proudly at the centre, staring the artist in the eye, Mama behind me, Aunt Betty behind Belle. Beside them, my dear father and Lord Mansfield respectively. My siblings around us: Frances with a book in her hand, Mary seated at the harpsichord, Kitty and Billy on the floor in each other's arms. It was a magnificent portrait.

Glasses were raised and clinked, and cheers went up all around. Mama took Papa's hand and led him towards the dancing.

By one of the windows stood Mary Robinson, watching the revels outside with a wry smile.

'All right girls!' she said, raising her glass to us.

'You know, Miss Robinson,' I said. 'There's something that we didn't get to the bottom of when we were trying to solve the Othello case.'

'Oh yes?' she asked, her eyes flashing with curiosity.

'You were so rattled when we interviewed you for *Stage Door* magazine, we thought you must be guilty of something . . .'

'Well, you said you were writing a column for *Stage Door*. One's got to protect one's livelihood, hasn't one? If you get my meaning!' She cast me a sly, sideways glance. 'That being said, there's plenty of room for all of us. You want to write, girls – you write! It's the best profession going! But . . .' she tapped the side of her nose, 'no one needs to know who that *mystery correspondent* is, do they? That's the point of being anonymous!'

Outside, Kitty and Billy had joined a group of children

who were rolling down the slopes at the back of the house. Down they tumbled after one another, their giggles disappearing into the darkness as they went. On the path up ahead, the silhouettes of Frances and Joshua as they walked slowly towards the rose garden. Frances looked so different from this distance. A young queen, head held high, resplendent in gold, with her man on her arm.

Belle and I strolled up to the crest of the highest hill – the viewpoint from which you could gaze down on the city in all its glory. The green fields rolled away from us, down, down to the fringe of dark trees that crouched at the Heath's edge.

In the velvet darkness, the moon illuminated the distant rooftops and the tiny spires with a gentle silver touch.

London. Our city. What secrets did it hold for us in the future?

'Belle, I have a gift for you!' I said, handing her a small package from my cloak pocket.

Carefully, Belle untied the ribbon and unwrapped the parcel. Inside was a handkerchief, handstitched with golden bells around the border. In the centre, a single quill.

'It's to say thank you for showing me how powerful the written word can be,' I said.

She sparkled with gratitude. 'Oh, Lizzie, it's beautiful! Thank you!'

'Don't lose it, whatever you do!'

She laughed and gave me a mischievous look. 'I have something for you, too!'

She took my hand and pressed something into it. A small visiting card, embossed in gold letters with the words:

Lizzie AND Belle

Agents of History, Partners in Mystery
Sisters in solving crime

Enquire at Sancho's Tea Shop, Westminster, or
post enquiries to Kenwood House,
Hampstead Heath, London

'I've had a set made,' she said with that characteristic shyness. 'Just in case . . .'

I grabbed her in a hug that Mama would have been proud of.

'You're brilliant, Belle!' I said. 'You really are the most amazing friend a girl could wish for.'

We stepped back from our hug and held each other's hands.

'Here's to the future of a fantastic friendship!' Belle declared.

Back at the house, the musicians were playing a superfast reel. The hall was whirling with circles of people holding hands and galloping round and round the room.

'Shall we?' I suggested.

We rushed in and joined the throng, dancing and spinning, dancing and spinning until I felt myself becoming giddier and giddier, my head light with excitement and happiness.

The spell was ruptured by an explosion of breaking glass, quickly followed by a high-pitched scream. The music faltered into silence. The dancers stumbled to a halt.

Suddenly everyone made for the door in a confusion of silk and satin. Cries and shouts of dismay pierced the darkness as we spilled out of the house on to the slope, a mass of silhouettes under the moonlight.

'What happened? Did anyone see anything?' Belle cried.

'Look!' someone shouted. 'The library!'

One of the library windows was shattered, a great arched hole in its place. Shards of glass sparkled dangerously in the moonlight on the pathway. A curtain billowed recklessly in the breeze.

Suddenly, out of the melee, my sister Frances, running towards us.

'Lizzie, Belle!' she said breathlessly, putting her hand on my shoulder to steady herself.

'It's our portrait! It's been stolen!'

A Note on
History and Fiction

The book you have just read is, as you know, a fiction: a work of the imagination. While some of the characters in this book are based on real people, others have been invented for the sake of the story.

Elizabeth Sancho and Dido Belle were real people who lived in London in the eighteenth century with their families. At that time, little was recorded of women's lives. Even less of Black lives. And still less of the lives of Black women and girls.

Yet more and more records of Black life in eighteenth-century London are coming to the surface all the time. More and more clues are emerging as evidence of a rich and varied Black presence in London. And all of those lives have their own story.

As far as we know, Ignatius Sancho never got to play Othello on stage as he wished. At the time of writing, we believe that Ira Aldridge, an African American actor, was the first Black man to play Othello in Britain when he appeared on the London stage in 1825, aged just 17. But as Ignatius suggests in this book, we can use our imaginations to help us to begin to think about our past – and our present, and our future – in new ways.

How do we learn our history? How do we come to know what we think we know about the past? Who decides what is important enough to write down and preserve for the future? Whose stories have been told in this way? And whose have been left out of the historical record?

These are questions that can help us to understand that history is not a fixed thing. The more we know about the past, the more our understanding of that past changes. History is fresh, living, breathing, constantly renewing itself. And sometimes, the first step into envisioning the past is a step into the imagination . . .

Acknowledgements

It takes a village to raise a child.

My heartfelt thanks to those who have helped me to bring Lizzie and Belle into the world!

To Jasmine Richards, Storymix founder, thanks for your powerful vision, your boundless energy and your unending encouragement. What a sister!

To Simone, thank you for seeing Lizzie and Belle as vividly I did and for bringing these girls and their world to life with such creativity, care and flair.

To Liz Bankes, Aleena Hasan, Lucy Courtenay, Olivia Adams and the team at Farshore, thanks for your fizzing enthusiasm and passion for this story, for a letter I shall never forget, and for your gentle guidance throughout this process.

To the pupils and students I have worked with over the years, thank you for showing me just how much fun being a teacher can be and the magic that happens when young people are given the space to think, to talk and to write about what matters to them.

My thanks to the writers and historians whose work has preceded, inspired and strengthened my own. No one of us is an island.

My thanks to my dear friends and family – you surrounded me with your love and support on this exciting journey during extraordinary times.

My profound gratitude to my own pride of lions: Richard, Felix, Frankie, whom I love more than I can express in words alone. This book is dedicated to you and to the memory of Margaret, my mother, who showed me how to find joy in even the darkest of moments and John, my father, who taught me that art, music and literature are for everyone. Their souls sparkle on in my heart, always.

Stage Door Interview with J.T. Williams

What made you want to become an author, and did your teaching experience play a part in this?

For me, books are a fierce and lifelong passion! As an only child I spent many hours reading: losing myself in worlds old and new, in the lives, adventures and emotions of other people. Reading wove a spell around me, transported me right into the heart of someone else's life and the inner workings of their mind.

I have always loved writing too. Since the age of twelve, I have kept diaries, scribbling down what I notice, what fascinates me. I also enjoy playing with words to bring imaginary experiences to life in depth and detail. Language is such a gift – I love the way words sound, their musicality!

I became a teacher because I wanted to share my passion for reading. I believe that it is everyone's right to be transported by words as I was – whether spoken or written, whether through song or poetry or stories. Language can connect us with so many different versions of the world. This is how we build empathy.

Now I write to invite people into the realm of my imagination. I craft stories to create new pathways into the past. It's never too late to become an author!

Why did you choose to write a mystery story? What is it about Lizzie and Belle as individuals that fit this genre?

The stories of Black people in Britain intrigue me. Though we have been here for centuries, many of our stories have been hidden for a long time. I love trying to find something that you know is there but remains hidden from you, that you have to work really hard to uncover – this is true of the work of the writer, of the historian, and of the detective! There is evidence of Black people's lives in Georgian Britain, but I want to know how people *felt*. What they thought about, what they worried about, what they got excited about. There are clues to these perspectives, but we have to fit the pieces together like a jigsaw puzzle. Sometimes we don't have all the answers, but that's where the imagination comes in!

How did you first hear about Dido Belle and Ignatius Sancho, and what was it about their experiences that captured your attention?

I grew up very close to Kenwood House. I've been walking on the Heath since I was about twelve years old. But I did not discover the story of Dido Belle until the copy of her portrait was hung at Kenwood in 2007. From that moment I was captivated! Here was a young woman of mixed heritage, just like me, staring out at me from this extraordinary painting, pointing to her dark skin with an enigmatic smile and a twinkle in her eye. What an invitation!

I discovered Sancho much later – only a few years ago, in fact. And as soon as I heard his incredible story – birth on a slave ship, growing up in the family of three sisters who mistreated him, running away and learning to read and write, becoming a composer, a letter-writer and a devoted husband and father – I just couldn't believe I had not known about him for so long. Then I read his letters and his voice just flew off the page and straight into my heart. To read those letters is to feel that this compassionate, funny, energetic, witty, joyful man is in the room, chatting to you directly. Such a vivid voice! And the portrait that Thomas Gainsborough painted of him – it's so dignified, and, like Dido's portrait, so intriguing.

Sancho was an orphan; and though Dido's parents were

alive, she did not live with them. I lost my parents before I became an adult, and I think I am very drawn to orphan stories, to experiences of orphanhood. It's a unique way of being in the world that is very hard to imagine if it is not your experience. But both Dido and Sancho derive a kind of strength and resilience from that experience. You carry your sadness, but you know that you have to be your own strongest person, to be your own mother and father to yourself, and there's something actually very empowering about realising that and carrying it with pride.

Did you always know you wanted both girls to be the main characters, or was there ever a possibility of just focusing on one character?

The Lizzie and Belle Mysteries were conjured out of a partnership with the wonderful Jasmine Richards at Storymix. We had talked about a story just involving Lizzie, and then we explored the idea of her working in partnership with Belle. As soon as we happened on that, the story started to run away with itself! The heart of these stories is the friendship that develops between these two extraordinary girls – each bringing their own special skills and magic to the mix. What better way to celebrate the spirit of collaboration!

Whose personality do you relate to more between Lizzie and Belle?

As a younger girl, I was tiny for my age, but strong and speedy. Maybe a bit cheeky, too? And I was really proud of being those things. But they didn't seem to be things that girls were expected to be, and I always found that odd. When I'm writing Lizzie, I'm very firmly back with my own sassy twelve-year-old self.

There are elements of Belle's experience that I share too. Perhaps from later in life. There is a part of me that believes that books can teach you anything you want to know about the world! And I do know what it is like to be that lone person looking in on larger families. There are so many facets of Belle that I relate to – but I won't share everything here. We'll be finding out more about Belle in book two!

Case notes for J.T. Williams

Identity: *Mystery writer with a passion for hidden histories, lifelong Londoner.*

Observed behaviours: *Fast talking, long-distance walking, daily dancing, relentless reading and writing.*

Top tips for sleuthing: *Listen with intensity. Notice everything. Keep connecting.*

Motive: *J.T. Williams writes to shine a spotlight on the Black British past. Blends fact with fiction by basing stories on the lives of real people. Passionate about the power of storytelling to give voice to those rarely heard. Walks the city streets to uncover its secrets.*

Mission: *To build a team of agents of history, partners in mystery, specialists in solving crime.*

Case notes for Simone Douglas

Identity: *90s baby, full-time artist, Londoner and adventure game protagonist.*

Observed behaviours: *Spotted out taking long walks, watching thrillers and enjoying classic cartoons and video games from her childhood.*

Top tips for illustrating: *Channel what you love into your art, and find inspiration from everything around you.*

Motive: *Simone Douglas sources much inspiration from a childhood rich with vibrant cartoons, video games and classic Disney; she loves all things nostalgic.*

Mission: *To share her love for environmental art, and bring life to characters within their worlds.*

THE
Lizzie AND Belle
MYSTERIES

PORTRAITS AND POISONING

It's a race against time as the two girls track
down a portrait stolen from Kenwood House.
What could the thief want with something
so personal?

Meanwhile, a poisoner is on the loose . . .

Coming soon!